PENGUIN BOOKS

GET A LIFE

Nadine Gordimer, who was awarded the Nobel Prize in Literature in 1991, is the author of thirteen novels, nine volumes of stories, and three nonfiction collections. She lives in Johannesburg, South Africa.

GET A LIFE

///

Nadine Gordimer

Penguin Books

PENGUIN BOOKS

Published by the Penguin Group
Penguin Group (USA) Inc., 375 Hudson Street, New York, New York 10014, U.S.A.
Penguin Group (Canada), 90 Eglinton Avenue East, Suite 700, Toronto,
Ontario, Canada M4P 2Y3 (a division of Pearson Penguin Canada Inc.)
Penguin Books Ltd, 80 Strand, London WC2R 0RL, England
Penguin Ireland, 25 St Stephen's Green, Dublin 2, Ireland (a division of Penguin Books Ltd)
Penguin Group (Australia), 250 Camberwell Road, Camberwell,
Victoria 3124, Australia (a division of Pearson Australia Group Pty Ltd)
Penguin Books India Pvt Ltd, 11 Community Centre, Panchsheel Park, New Delhi – 110 017, India
Penguin Group (NZ), cnr Airborne and Rosedale Roads, Albany,
Auckland 1310, New Zealand (a division of Pearson New Zealand Ltd)
Penguin Books (South Africa) (Pty) Ltd, 24 Sturdee Avenue,
Rosebank, Johannesburg 2196, South Africa

Penguin Books Ltd, Registered Offices:
80 Strand, London WC2R 0RL, England

First published in the United States of America by Farrar, Straus and Giroux 2005
Published in Penguin Books 2006

10   9   8   7   6   5   4   3   2   1

THE LIBRARY OF CONGRESS HAS CATALOGED THE HARDCOVER EDITION AS FOLLOWS:
Gordimer, Nadine.
Get a life / by Nadine Gordimer.
p.   cm.
ISBN-13: 978-0-374-16170-5 (hc.)
ISBN-10: 0-374-16170-4 (hc.)
ISBN 0 14 30.37927 7 (pbk.)
1. Ecologists—Fiction.   2. Quarantine—Fiction.   3. Cancer—Patients—Fiction.
4. Cancer—Treatment—Fiction.   5. Ecologists—Family relationships—Fiction.   I. Title.
PR9369.3.G6G48 2005
823'.914—dc22   2005007199

Printed in the United States of America
Designed by Dorothy Schmiderer Baker

Reinhold

2005

O what authority gives

Existence its surprise?

—W. H. Auden,

"The Sea and the Mirror"

Contents

i / *Child's Play*

Only the street-sweeper swishing his broom to collect fallen leaves from the gutter.

The neighbours might have seen, but in the middle of a weekday morning everyone would be out at work or away for other daily-life reasons.

She was there, at the parents' driveway gate as he arrived, able to smile for him, and quickly sense the signal for them to laugh at, accept the strangely absurd situation (only temporary) that they could not hug one another. A foregone hug is less emotional than a foregone embrace. Everything is ordinary. The sweeper passes pushing the summer's end before him.

Radiant.

Literally radiant. But not giving off light as saints are shown with a halo. He radiates unseen danger to others from a destructive substance that has been directed to counter what was destroying him. Had him by the throat. Cancer of the thyroid gland. In hospital he was kept in isolation. Even that of silence; he had no voice for a while, mute. Vocal cords affected. He remains, he will be still, out of his control, exposing others and objects to what he emanates, whomever and whatever he touches.

Everything must be ordinary.

Calling from one car window to the other: Has she remembered his laptop? Some cassettes? His Adidas? The book on the behaviour of relocated elephants he was in the middle of reading when he went back to hospital? Berenice—Benni— why do parents burden their children with fancy names— has packed a bag for him. She wept while she made decisions on his behalf, put this in, take that out. But she not only remembered; familiarity knew what he would need, miss. In one of the books he will find she has slipped a photograph of herself he liked particularly, he'd taken before their love affair turned into marriage. There's a snap of the boy as a baby.

His mother fetched him from the hospital. He opened a door of the rear seat of the car, to sit in there, right from the start he must begin to follow a certain conduct of himself, make it a habit for the time being, but his mother is like him (if that's not a reverse order of inherited characteristics), she has decided on her own code of conduct in response to the threat he represents. She leans to open the door of the passenger seat beside her and pats it authoritatively.

He has a wife and child.

Whose life, whose risk is worth less than these?

Parents are responsible for bringing into the world their progeniture whether deliberately or carelessly and theirs is an unwritten covenant that the life of the child, and by descent the child's child, is to be valued above that of the original progenitors.

So Paul—that's him, the son—he has come home—oh differently, for the time being, yes—to the old home, that of his parents.

Lyndsay and Adrian are not old. The ladder of ageing has extended since medical science, sensible exercise, healthy diet have enabled people to linger longer and younger before ascending to disappear in the mystery at the top. ('Passing away' is the euphemism, but to where?) Unthinkable that the son is preceding, ahead of them, up there. His father is about to retire at a vigorous sixty-five from managing directorship of an agricultural vehicle and equipment plant. His mother, fifty-nine looking forty-nine, a longtime natural beauty with no wish for face-lifts, is considering whether or not she should leave her partnership in a legal practice and join her other partner in this new phase of existence.

The dog jumps and paws at him, sniffs the cold hospital pungency of his bulging hold-all and the delivered suitcase with what his wife anticipated his needs might be here, in this phase of his existence. —Which room? — It is not his old room, it's his sister's that has been turned into a study where his father will follow whatever interests he's supposed to have in readiness for retirement. This sister and brother born only twelve months apart due to excessive youthful passion or a mistaken reliance on the contraceptive efficacy of breast-feeding—Lyndsay still laughs at her ignorance and the opportunism of quick breeding! There are two other sisters, better biologically spaced. He has no brother.

He's unique.

The pestilent one, the leper. The new leper, that's it, how he thinks of himself, sardonically flip. His resort comes probably from the advertising fraternity/sorority's facility with turn of phrase he's picked up in the company of Benni's colleagues.

Paul Bannerman is an ecologist qualified academically at universities and institutions in the USA, England, and by experience in the forests, deserts, and savannahs of West Africa and South America. He has a post with a foundation for conservation and environmental control, in this country of Africa in which he was born; an employee presently on extended leave for health reasons. Benni/Berenice is a copywriter, advanced to management in one of the international advertising companies whose campaigns operate all over the world and whose name is globally familiar as a pop star's, keeping its form without need for translation, part of every language's vocabulary. She earns more than he does, of course, but that's no matter for imbalance in the mating since the role-casting of male as the provider is outdated, as the price of feminist freedom. It is probably the contrast in the context and different practices of their working lives that keeps for them a sense of the unknown, even sexually, that usually gets lost in habit after a few years of marriage. Familiarity; if she knew him well enough to anticipate his common needs learnt in five years of intimacy, this did not mean his comprehension of what the world is, how it functions, his intuitions, were not different from hers. Always something to talk about, a frustration, an achievement to trade, always the element of the stranger, each perceiving something, with the third eye, in the orbit of the other.

When the verdict came from the specialist oncologist through the general practitioner who was of their generation and in their group of friends, she was the one who answered the early morning call. Every day he left their bed first, accustomed to early rising on fieldwork. He came from the bathroom and found her pressed back against the pillows with tears leaking down her cheeks as if something inside her had suddenly given way. He stopped at the open door. Before he could speak she told him. There is no looking for the delay of an appropriate time for such ... what? News, information.

—It's cancer. The thyroid. Bad. Jonathan couldn't make it sound anything else.— The dissolve ran down to her lips, trembled on her chin.

He stood there. His mouth stirred, as if about to speak. Stood, alone. Such news belongs only to the one from whose body the message has come. Then he closed the mouth in a tight line, distortion of a smile in some attempt at recognition of her presence.

—Well. Could get run over by a bus. You have to die sometime.—

Freshly shaven, his face shone in the slicked suntan of a week's trip in the coastal wetlands from which he'd returned a few days ago, ignoring the wait for doctors' decision on the result of tests.

But at thirty-five! Where had it come from? No cancer in his family health records! Nothing! Healthy childhood, no illnesses—how? Why? She could not stop herself gabbling accusations.

He sat down on the bed beside the shape of her legs under the blankets. Moved his head in denial, not despair, for a moment, then got up automatically purposeful and pulled his trousers over the minuscule underpants that held—unaffected, that end, anyway—his manhood. While he dressed and she lay there he asked his questions. —So what did Jonathan say is to be done?— He didn't continue, but everyone knows that doctors, even your close buddy, won't pronounce a clear death sentence.

—They'll operate. Should be right away.—

Both were confronted with what would be the evidence to challenge, postpone whatever this mutilation was going to be: look at the man, the clear architrave of the rib cage containing the rise and fall of life-breath beneath the muscular pads of pectorals, the smooth hard contour of biceps, the strong lean forearms—nature's complete evolutionary construction for all functions. There's a pretty phrase for it that's obsolete: the picture of health.

He could not avoid her holding his presence as if keeping a statue in vision while he strapped on his watch, went about

the business of dressing. The victim is led to the scaffold—
there are doctors to do it if there are no jailers—without the
one who loves him. That one shut out. He must do something
for her. He turned back to where she lay, bent to put his arms
round her against the soft give of the pillows and kissed each
wet cheek. But she pulled her hands free roughly and seizing
his head pushed his mouth hard against hers, opened his lips
with a stiff tongue and the kiss was about to become a passionate prelude when the child was heard demanding from
the adjoining room, calling, calling. He lifted himself from
her, they awkwardly disentangled and she ran barefoot to
answer the insistent summons of the life they had passed on
some night from an embrace in this bed.

Everything evolves into what has to be done next. There
were more specialist consultations, more laboratory tests and
the wise men in surgeons' white coats, if not wizards reading
the firmament or sangomas reading the bones, made their
decisions. All one had to do, oneself, was comply, present
one's body. It belonged to the men in white coats (in fact, one
of the specialists is female, so the body is taken over by a
woman in a manner never before, asexual. Not something in
a healthy young male's experience!) While the preliminary
processes for surgery were going on, he and the real woman,
Benni, made love every night. Only at night, and in this way,
could fear bury itself. The unbelievable become one flesh.

Her own parents were divorced and both farther and further separated by the seas between the Southern and Northern Hemispheres; she did not know whether to write to one

or both about what had invaded her—the dread, certainty— she put off the attempt at composition of such a letter. Her mother flying back to the country of her outlived past to support her daughter—the idea brought recoil at the vision of the airport where that composite figure of childhood and absence would appear. Her father, there he was reading out to his third wife the letter of this daughter from a failed episode in his life who had made—he'd decide?—his way of dealing with it—an unfortunate marriage to some fellow who turned out to be seriously ill at thirty-something.

Lyndsay and Adrian. His parents. *The* parents. Benni had to admit to herself and the few intimate friends to whom she was willing to disclose what had fallen upon Paul like the wrath of an Almighty neither he nor she believed in—his parents were marvellous. Although he was their son, she and Paul had had an even relationship to them, he didn't see them more intimately, or more often than he and she did together and mainly on occasions of family gatherings, the birthdays, Christmas, a treat out at a restaurant or round the table, siblings and their attachments, where he and his sisters had grown up; the next generation, the grandchildren, urged to play together because they were something called cousins. No closeness to his parents, really. But now as if there were a normal course of events to be provided for in closeness, Lyndsay and Adrian offered—went ahead and made—practical arrangements the son and his wife had no thought for. Lyndsay absented herself from chambers of the legal firm where her name was one of So-and-So & Partners and took charge of the child, fetching him from playschool to care for him for the end of each day in the house where his father had run about at this same lively age, while Benni, her clients, computers, and copywriters left to others, accompanied Paul to the waiting rooms of clinics and pathology laboratories where the pre-operative test rituals were performed.

After recovery from surgery, thyroidectomy's the scientific term, he was allowed to go back to the ordinary: Benni, the small son, work. Recovery: an interim four weeks while an obligatory period passed before the radioactive iodine treatment the doctors had found, by means of a scan, was necessary to what's their word, ablate residual cancerous tissue. He, and Benni and his parents under the unspoken sacred authority of the life-threatened one, lived the four weeks as if they were the usual progress of daily preoccupations. Ordinary. He timed a field trip that brought him from the wilderness the day before he presented himself back at the hospital for this ablation process.

He and his wife were told, in the most tactful way such Outer Space instructions may be conveyed, that when he was discharged after a few days of total isolation in hospital he still would be radioactive and a threat to those in contact with him. His wife came to tell Adrian and Lyndsay, who were together in the family home, the old house. It was not for a moment necessary to wonder what to do. Lyndsay spoke at once, for both of them, and it was there, in the tightening of Adrian's forehead and his darkly fixed eye, that she was certainly so doing. —He'll come to us. Until it's safe.—

Taken for granted.

It would have been somehow intrusive to bring up the risk to them; clearly that final of all matters, the value of life and death, had long been discussed ultimately and privately, and resolved between them. Don't break down in emotion of gratitude. What decision other than this should she have expected a mother and father make? What conception of their own parenthood did their son and his wife have, then.

Only when they saw her off at her car did she turn without knowing what she was doing or as if to pick up some object left behind, and put her arms round Adrian, her head coming only to the level of his chest, a first-time embrace after five years of the peck on either cheek at Christmas and birthdays. Then to Lyndsay, two women touching breast-to-breast for a moment. The three had not spoken to one another on the walk from the house to the car. The last exchange had been as Adrian stood back to let the women pass through the front door: he had asked when was the probable date of Paul's discharge, and she had told him maybe two days, still.

Lyndsay's spread hand shaded her eyes from the sun. —Well, soon as you know . . . I'll fetch him from the hospital.— Only logical, she was already committed to being in contact with whatever it was that he would represent.

Benni with slow precision contained, restrained herself with the seat belt, turned the key in the ignition, slotted the gear, released the brake. Nothing else for her. The car had automatic transmission, at once moving over the gravel with the sound that came to her as grit grinding between clenched teeth, the doors snapped locked. Shut out of the process that was taking him over, herself detained in the prison of safety. She could not imagine what this kind of isolation would be like. For the first time since she took the call with his diagnosis, she was thinking not of him but of herself, herself. If there had been tears now as she drove they would have been for her.

The house is listening. Every now and then it is interrupted by the hum of the refrigerator turning itself on to maintain its ski resort temperature in the warm kitchen. He meant to get up and appear at breakfast with them but the doctors hadn't wanted to discourage him by telling him how deathly tired he would feel even after excusing himself to get to bed early and sleeping eight hours. His limbs, those biceps and forearms, thighs and calves, would not move. He could not even tremble into effort; there was no summoning it.

You just rest. Adrian's face round the door, stealthily, speaking only when he saw the son's eyes open. Lyndsay jostling from behind. That's what recuperation is. The parents had decided his state was recuperation. This was a better attitude than the doctors' informed conviction that tests would monitor whether removal of the gland and the blinding dazzle of invading radioactive iodine would defeat the opportunism of predatory cells to show a renewed attack elsewhere; congratulated themselves that the vocal cords had not been seriously damaged. The patient speaks in a normal voice, not like some sort of castrato, even the timbre is his own. When he thinks in this dim-dozing timeless half-consciousness lying in bed, of what must have been done to him while he was totally absent in an operating theatre, he watches a few maverick cells dartingly escaping the knife, later fleeing the radiant iodine to set up a new base in what he experiences is the territory of his body. It's a car-chase movie of the kind he'd switch from to another channel. The doctors have been pleased to note that the sense of humour he produces before them is a positive factor, the right spirit to endure whatever is ahead for him according to the oracle of the scan.

The parents have gone, she to So-and-So & Partners' chambers with a sheaf of documentation of her current case, he to his board meeting.

Lyndsay has arranged the 'quarantine' with the object of making him, Adrian, and her least embarrassed and aware of it. She has a special basket, souvenir of one of her trips years ago to a legal conference in a country where one bought such craft at the airport and didn't know to what use to put it, that was now the repository for his clothes and bed linen to be set aside for washing separately from the general bundle done by Primrose. One of those supermarket compartmented plastic trays held his cutlery kept apart with glasses and cups in a cupboard cleared of kitschy gifts, detritus of house guests, that it seemed wrong to throw away but never used. Plates: it would have been an unnecessary waste (sacrifice) to destroy, after the recuperation, as a necessary precaution, crockery with the beautiful hand-painted motifs from Italy she had ordered in some inexplicable fit of extravagance one year. (Who could have dreamed then, in that exquisite place, that a time would come for a different kind of hyperbole to describe expenses that were far exceeding medical aid schemes.) She had stocked a supply of barbecue paper plates of the kind stout enough to hold hot food. Adrian, through an industrialist friend with—no doubt—doubtful influence over the network people, had promptly installed a telephone and fax line in the assigned room, in fact right there, a stretched hand away, on a bedside table.

He could call Benni. At work. Or on her mobile if she's driving; is she wearing the no-hands model with the ear-aperture attachment he insisted on buying for her when the only thought for exposure to radiation likely to affect them was that said to exist in the old models clamped to the head. He cannot lift the hand, no device of the millennial gods of communication could reach across infinitude between how he lies and the module console-desks, Corbusier lookalike chairs, leather sofas for clients, professional flower arrangements, blown-up images of improbably beautiful or famous people and landscape paradises, from award-winning advertising campaigns; Berenice is admirably successful. A fax—to whom? His team, Thapelo and Derek, stick figures in the area where the intention to site a pebble-bed nuclear reactor plant has to be opposed. When he was in a wilderness her city place did not exist for him, as at her console in that city space his wilderness did not exist for her.

Neither does. Both equally unreachable. He's the receded. It's him. Far away.

Planes can land on automatic pilot. He's got up and gone

to the bathroom reserved for him. Radiation is carried in urine and faeces. As he pees it just occurs to him, will he ever wake up with an erection again.

They have not left him really alone. There's the servant, now called housekeeper. Except that he's alone, apart, with anybody—everyone. His mind continues haphazard ridiculous wanderings; dogs are put in quarantine quarters, for months, when taken to other countries, a precaution against carrying rabies infection from Africa. Poor doggie. For him, the doctors have said, about sixteen days, including the first few in hospital isolation. Enough. Then he'd be fine, clear.

First they'd assured that the removal of the gland would be all that was necessary for a cure, he'd be fine, clear.

Then they'd had to admit that sometimes residual thyroid tissue remained after surgery. Could be intentional—to continue something of the normal function of the thyroid gland; sometimes inadvertent. Which was the case in his instance was not volunteered and what was the point of questioning anyway.

Neither his wife nor the parents were aware that of course he knew about the treatment for residual malignant tissue before the doctors told him and his wife. After the announcement by telephone of what had him by the throat, an early morning in the bedroom, he had gone that day to the university medical school and said he was doing research which required use of a medical library. There he had his own consultation with documentation on papillary carcinoma, the most serious form of thyroid cancer. More frequent in women and in both sexes more frequent in the young. So: thirty-five, a candidate. Read on. If there is suspicion that after thyroidectomy some tissue remains, then radioactive iodine ablation must follow. This radioactive iodine treatment is dangerous to others who come into contact with the individual who has received it.

Iodine, the innocent stuff dabbed on a child's scratched knee.

A few weeks' isolation. Fine, clear. Now sure the assurance, again, this time.

He would have to know, from within.

Primrose (it's not only whites who dub their offspring with pretentiously inappropriate names, a queen in ancient times, a flower in the imagined gardens from which the rich conquerors came) has left his breakfast prepared according to new household instructions. Tea and toast on an electric hot tray, fruit and yoghurt, honey, a cereal he doesn't know still existed, must have been something his mother remembered in connection with him as a child. A spoonful tastes like hay.

Primrose who knows him, of course, from ordinary occasions visiting the parents, does not appear. Through the windows open to let in the morning sun (what time is it, does a watch really know) there comes a low busy conversational twitter. He used to have budgerigars in a cage in this house as a kid, they would communicate confidentially like that—Lyndsay, his mother, who couldn't bear to have creatures caged, communicated the realisation of the birds' imprisonment to him. He must have given them away. But this low morning conversation was not that of caged birds but Primrose and some friends passing whatever the time was for them. He had not been told of the problem of Primrose as a member of the household. Realised it only as he ate the food prepared by her and heard her, unseen, in the cadence of African voices speaking their own language.

Adrian and Lyndsay had had to decide what to do, whether this woman, innocent of danger, innocent of any family responsibility towards the son, should be exposed at all. Lyndsay woke up in the night after a long discussion earlier and spoke aloud as if it were continuing. Adrian stirred and said the right thing she hadn't taken into account, as he so often did. (So much for her legal mind.) They must speak to Primrose: the decision to send her away must not be seen as a banishment from her place in their lives but come about with her full understanding and acceptance as their duty to her safety.

The tall heavy woman, ageing gourd filled with a life of many troubles, rather than a delicate yellow flower, who had never before been called into the livingroom to sit down and talk with her employers, nevertheless gave them the uninhibited attention their good relations, her considerate working conditions and excellent pay, she found naturally called for. The white people didn't try any of the sentimental coming close many did with blacks these days when they wanted something from you, the mama didn't start off with the you-are-a-mother-yourself bit. And there was no father for the dad to claim as a father like himself; the man who had fathered Tembisa, the boy for whose education at a private school the employers were paying—had long gone back to his wife in the Transkei. First Adrian explained in detail Paul's illness, treatment, and this strange aftermath unlike that of any other illness. When she didn't follow, she pinched her mouth, lifted her cheeks to their high bones and asked: What—what. It was both a question and horrified compassion; of course she had enquired, every day, for news of his condition while he was in hospital, shaking her head, God will see he comes through. They had to explain, while not offending this faith, that he had not come quite through, not yet. Once she had heard the facts there was little need to explain why he could not go home to his young wife and child. She pre-empted them. —He must come here to us.— Didn't they know she had enjoyed sharing the care of the little boy when Mama was in charge while the mother was busy with the doctors and the husband?

There was the proposal, she would go to her home in the new government housing scheme in the district where she was born, a house they had, in fact, helped her, with a gift of the down-payment, to build for her mother.

—How long.—

They did not know. Adrian reassured her; she would have her full wages.

She brooded, a pause they respected without offering a repetition of explanations.

—Take a little holiday.— Adrian tried again.

She addressed Lyndsay, there are considerations men, who everywhere, at her mother's house or this one, have everything done for them, do not understand. —How you can manage?—

Lyndsay gave a small grunt of a laugh. —I don't know. But I will.—

And now to Adrian, the man. —Her work every day and the papers she bring to read at night. I see the light on late.—

How can you manage meant: I do not go. So then there were three in concentrated discussion, like complicity. How could she stay? Was it possible to arrange her presence, as they had arranged the study for quarantine tenancy; ensure that her duties would entail the absolute minimum of contact with danger from touch, clothing, utensils—who knows about the air breathed.

But all was accepted on some unspoken understanding that they—the mama and her husband—were allowing her to put herself at risk along with them, the only ones who had reason to. Perhaps the woman had survived so much in her life that she couldn't really believe in the danger they couldn't say came only from a cough, from a person's shit, from pus or blood. Something he gave off, some kind of light you couldn't see.

What do you do when you have no purpose, are allowed no purpose but something his mother has called 'recuperate'. As good a term as any other euphemism for—whatever. You can call up anything you want on the Internet, what about this? He could not really believe he was going to have to die, rogue cells were moving around right now within the territory of himself; dying is a remote business, has no reality when you are in your thirties, all that can happen is you're run over by a bus. Shot by a hijacker. His work is scientific, in collaboration with the greatest scientist of all, nature, who has the formula for everything, whether discovered or still a mystery to research by its self-styled highest creation; in that university library, naturally, he'd read up everything about the thyroid gland, that hidden nodule in your neck he could put a hand up to feel for, if it hadn't been removed. It is a vital factor in growth along with the pituitary, which is hidden behind your forehead, he wouldn't have come to adolescence, physical and mental maturity, without it. These sites should be marked like the sacred signals coloured on the brows of Hindus. So, demonstrably, the gland has an effect on emotions aside from its necessary physical manifestations if it decides to go erratic, an excess of thyroid gland production causes tachycardia, a rapid heartbeat. Some even aver a connection between excessive thyroid activity and creative ability in the arts—the imagination is accelerated, too. You take it that your type of intelligence is decided by the size and composition of your brain—that's it. But there are these other little pockets of substances whose alchemy influences, and interferes—even directly—in what you *are.* Many other abstruse details about the component now missing from his neck, a scar at the spot where it once secretly functioned and where the cells turned rogue in crazy proliferation. He's able to meet doctors almost on their own informed scientific ground, so to speak, and what he's wanted to know from early on when he was told the gland must be removed, is what his life would be without it. He was told not to worry, let's just beat the cancer. You'll take some routine medication. And that is? Oh something called Eltroxin, substitutes for the thyroid's function, very well.

Back in his allotted room he hears someone else's human bustle, with him out of the way the woman is running a vacuum cleaner somewhere. There is the stereo equipment set up by his father and the cassettes Benni didn't forget. Surely there is no purposelessness the music you love cannot deny by the act of your listening. There's the elephant study and other books you never have time enough to read. The laptop computer. Briefcase of papers to collate and write up from the St Lucia wetlands research with Thapelo and Derek. And the telephone. What will there be to say to the person at the other end.

What do you do when you have no obligation, no everyday expectation of yourself and others?

You get out of where you are. Leave the walls of gaping emptiness behind. His feet took the way used in childhood, through the deep windows in the livingroom, to the garden. A man was loosening a bed round shrubs, the tines of a heavy fork biting into firm ground with each heave, he paused halfway in a movement and raised a hand in the kind of greeting salute a black worker is expected to give a white man, he completed the rhythm of his half-movement and the fork sounded his effort and the earth's resistance to it. Someone with a purpose.

The big woman came round from the back of the house, the usual woollen cap askew on her head cockily ridiculing the prissy English 'Primrose'. —You all right? Everything okay?—

Across the width of the lawn, for her safety, he thanked her for breakfast, showing off his smattering of Zulu, the only African language he'd usefully acquired for work in rural areas, thought by whites to be some kind of African lingua franca. The attempt was almost a connection with his working, functioning life. She laughed. —My pleasure. My pleasure.— Along with 'Have a nice day', conditioned formulae everywhere in divided worlds to bring policies of reconciliation to an everyday level of polite convention. As an unbeliever unthinkingly will respond 'Bless you' to someone who sneezes. The new demotics have reached even this one, an old-fashioned black woman, no dreadlocks, no railway tracks woven with the hair on her head, no topknot of yellow-dyed false curls he's familiar with among the beautiful sister-executives in Berenice's advertising agency, or the elegant secretaries, high-breasted and nose in the air, in the government offices his work takes him to. The phone is ringing from the room he left, but when he gets there to lift the receiver the caller has hung up.

Immeasurable tide of weariness has come back. He is lying on the bed again when later the call is loud beside him. It is Benni. —I tried you earlier—

—I was in the garden.—

—Oh good.—

Lyndsay and Adrian cancelled their cruise to the Arctic Wondrous Northern Lights *aurora borealis* and fortunately it's apparent neither Paul nor Berenice remembered it was planned, so there were no protestations necessary to convince anyone that this was of no account. The trip had been Adrian's idea because he sensed that his Lyn was in two minds about what that ominous state, retirement, would mean, supposing she joined him in it, and the fact of choosing to go somewhere, now, some remote travel they'd never thought of, would show that ventures could be part of the new state. This journey, from the extreme of the Southern Hemisphere to the extreme of the Northern, would convey that without need of words between them. Just as she must know he loved her, still even desired her, as he did when they first began to live together.

The parents tried to avoid going out in the evenings without making it too obvious that they were staying at home because of him. When there was a concert with a programme

Adrian particularly wanted to hear—his pleasure in Penderecki, Cage, and Philip Glass came from an eclectic depth of understanding she envied as beyond her—he went, she stayed at home with Paul. And in a way that was a treat, when last had mother and son the chance to spend an evening alone together. The small boy, the adolescent one mustn't intrude upon too closely, emotions must turn away from the one woman to other women, the young man with whom there had been adult friendship and understanding of one another—these had become the man with a wife and child. Now alone they spoke mostly of his work and how he felt about it—privately, essential to his being—as probably she thought he did only with his woman, his wife. His almost angry dedication, there were so many forces, political, economic, against it, had essential dependent connections with her work in the law that they had never really discussed before. The question of how, which rivers and seas should be exploited is decided ultimately by laws promulgated by governments. Paul and Thapelo and Derek might prove that this form of exploitation in a particular environment may be managed with benefit to human, animal, organic growth and the atmosphere; that form, in another environment will sicken the human population with effluent, starve animal species of their food habitat, take more from the sea than it can replace. But the 'findings' of ecological research by government-approved project entrepreneurs are produced as some sort of justification in going ahead with their projects. Never mind the independent researchers (the Pauls and Thapelos and Dereks) who prove otherwise; their findings can be given token attention, oh yes, the enterprise projects doctored up a bit as a concession—and the disastrous proceeds. So environmentalists have need of consultation with lawyers who know what loopholes, under the law, used by project entrepreneurs, must be anticipated and exposed while independent research is in progress.

Consultations like this one under quarantine. He's not allowed alcohol and when she forgets, in the mingle of their voices become familiar again, and says, let's have a glass of wine, she quickly corrects: no, I'll put the kettle on, what about camomile tea. He's smiling and lightly moving his head, you have your red wine, and she tips her head to match his movement, smiling refusal.

Her son is so exhausted by what they have both entered in intimacy that he has to go to bed before his father has returned from the concert.

There are other emanations than those she had been exposed to in a tête-à-tête. There are individuals for whom music moves on with its oxygen like the circulation of blood in the body and the brain, after it has been heard. Adrian came back in this serenely heightened state. It does not result from the kind of music you can hum, that she knew before he introduced her to something that opened her perceptions. People give one another things that can't be gift-wrapped. But she had not experienced the music with him tonight, not even at the level she could have expected with Penderecki and Cage. He read a little while beside her, one of the autobiographies unburdening the ugliness of the political past which they handed to one another to applaud or argue about.

They had already said what there was to exchange about

the evening at home. —How'd it go, was he all right.—
—It was good, I think he forgot . . .— —Not easy to talk,
I know.— —No, we talked. About his work just as if he's in
the middle of it.—

It was not the time to ruin the possibility of sleep by
speaking of what this brought to mind, was never out of
mind: would he ever take up that work again.

She lay with her eyes closed, somewhere trying to pace
her breathing along with that beside her as she would keep
up with his longer stride on walks. He put aside the book,
turned off the light. It was their long custom to dismiss the
day for each other by saying goodnight in the dark. The kiss
put a seal to it or led to lovemaking. He'd had some prostate
trouble but didn't need Viagra. The kiss tonight was a seal.

As he fell asleep he woke startlingly and heard her heav-
ing with sobs. For a confused moment it was as if he found
she was being attacked, desperate intruders know how to
defuse suburban burglar alarms. His hand struck the wall,
found the light switch. There was no-one. Her brutally self-
distorted face cringed at the glare. He turned it off and he
and the dark took her in his arms. Her body was hot, thick
and strange against him.

—Why did it have to be like this for him, so we could talk.
Talk. Why not before? What were we doing. Waited for this.
What happened to us. What's the matter with me so it couldn't
be these years that've been going by so satisfied with what
was supposed to be loving.—

—Lyn—my darling—you're doing everything. Everything
possible. Good God, you come home and make his bed, clean
his room, wash his clothes—his nurse, servant—taken on

more risk than anyone, than I do—all right, I helped him bath when he was still so weak—but how many professional women would get down to what you're doing.—

Her body began to shake as sobs made her choke and cough.

—Taking care of the man as you did when he was a baby. What more could there be. Listen to me, listen—

He stroked her hair, her shoulder, at last she scrubbed her face with the sheet and it came to him as a signal they would have to meet, kiss. While they entered each other by the silenced mouths he began to hold and fondle her breasts and a desperate desire rose in both of them. They made love, as Paul and his woman had buried their fear when the judgment came by telephone, and they were not aware of their son without this resort, this brief haven from fearful solitude. Just down the passage, where he had come home.

It turned out to be real that the inconceivable can become routine. At least so far as contact is decreed. Relationships. Their new nature, frequency, and limits. So if he does not get up to eat breakfast with them in the morning—sometimes too early a reminder that when he does join them his plate is paper and the utensils he uses must be put aside separately by Lyndsay or Adrian before they leave for the day—they make it their habit to open his door for an affectionate word of goodbye he knows is actually to see unobtrusively what state he's woken in. He supposes he must keep out of the kitchen as much as he can, although it's necessary, during the day when Primrose is not there, to go in for water or a snack from the refrigerator. While he eats his breakfast or lunch he may call out in a little exchange with Primrose attendant there beyond the door, asking what she's cooking up that smells so great, and receiving through the hearty gabble and thudding pop music of one of the African language radio stations she plays as she works, her dramatic report of the latest holdup she just heard about in a news flash. —These devils! Who were their mothers? God will punish them.— And with an effortless change of subject to the news of the progress of Tembisa in school sport—she wants to find something to tell that will interest a young man. Then she and the radio are gone.

Berenice calls as soon as she gets to her advertising agency every morning. Or from her mobile if she's on her way to a working breakfast where she's to outline a campaign to an important client. *Berenice.* He visualises her by that name, as represented her to him when they first met and like most people tentatively attracted to one another used calls to pursue the attraction between meetings.

This call is supposed to be a substitute for the natural exchange of daily preoccupations and happenings they've had since living together, that's the premise both must keep up. She has to fill the silences by relating what's in progress in her working life in diverting detail as if giving a report to an interested party—another, an intimate kind of client; he has nothing much at all to say.

Yesterday I listened to the whole *Fidelio*.

This morning?

Maybe the garden.

Well, nice place to read, looks like a lovely clear day. Enjoy!

Some mornings she has as a hang-up conclusion, awkwardly irrelevant, I love you.

Benni, by contrast, comes often and regularly in the afternoons. This is Benni, all right. In her unconventional, gypsy form of business dress and scarves she carries off so well and that he likes to watch her arming herself with when she gets up from their bed to begin a day. He watches her now as they stand in that No-Man's-Land, the safety of the garden, and unbidden, inappropriate, nerves coming alive from some anaesthesia, he has the surging yearning to touch her. Cross the few feet of space between them, where they stand, or where on the chairs from the terrace he's put out they sit, apart, facing each other; feel her under his hand. She has rung at the gate on the intercom, he has pressed the remote control, she has driven up the drive and he has been there, not far, not near, as she gets out of the car, and they stop—each held back. A greeting across the void, laughing, had they forgotten the sheer pleasure in seeing one another? But it has no natural conclusion in touch. This gap she hastens to fill with the things she has brought, more books, clothes, letters—once flowers, but that, both saw, was a mistake, as if he were a sick friend in hospital. Who can say what his existential category really is?

His mother takes him to the hospital for his out-patient monitoring. His father substitutes if the appointments coincide with a court hearing at which she is appearing for a client but he is not as familiar with the medical procedures as she is, which makes her uneasy—one cannot know the bond the unfamiliarity makes, the father and son entering, as two men, the alienation of the one, the way men bond in the traditionally male circumstances of war. Or, in another kind of gender identity, when (vividly again present, in the hospital waiting room) the ten-year-old boy and the father were side by side like this in homage to the physical power of maleness

at a rugby game. His father is Adrian, a man: this consciousness has become ignored under the filial relationship taking
second place to that with wife and child. Sitting beside him
in the nowhere of waiting rooms, the man knows that to look
at your woman across space and to be held back from going
over to touch her, breathe her, is a castrating frustration.

On the first weekend she brought their child to him, but
later visits had to be confined to the three-year-old boy seeing his father from the other side of the iron-barred gate—
he could not be stopped from running up to hug round his
father's legs, in an open encounter. And then there came the
day he flew into a tearful, violent rage, weeping as he clutched
the bars and yelling, Daddy, Daddy, *Paul*, Daddy, *Paul*. The
one called upon had to go away into the house so that the
child could be persuaded, in despair, to let go of the quarantine bars. No one of the adults who had brought him there to
visit his father could reach the depth in him that was perhaps
sure he would never see his father again.

It was decided not to expose the child to trauma while
protecting him from danger he could not be expected to understand. Instead his mother substituted for the sight of him
by beginning to talk a great deal about him, when she called,
and when she was a visitor at a distance. How their baby (still
was that) had had his first swimming lesson (there are many
dangers to be anticipated), how cross he'd become when a
friend from nursery school came to spend the night and wet
the bed, how he'd developed a passion for avocados and would
eat a whole one like an apple. Once she brought a crayon
drawing—he said it's for you. There's the home every child
draws, high walls, two windows, door, steep roof. A few
strokes as birds in the sky. A free-floating flower with trailing

kite-stems. His father had once bought a Chinese paper dragon and taken him out to fly it one Saturday afternoon but he was too young to understand how to control it. To the left and in the foreground, reaching up the picture higher than the house, a man with stick arms but carefully outlined pants, Chaplin-splayed feet, has a big head and huge bared teeth. Greeting? Or anger.

Primrose called to him at his breakfast, Why Nickie doesn't come to see his daddy no more? And the wail: Oh shame. But you must tell, you coming back soon, children don't think time like we do.

He had the impulse to bring the drawing from his bedside, where he had avoided looking at it since placing it where it ought to be, and he held it up for her to see from the distance of the kitchen door.

Adrian and Lyndsay manage the weekends well. It has never needed to be discussed, goes without saying that they refuse to keep their distance from him; even so far as that would be possible, sharing what's become the family house again. The only exception is that Lyndsay, the one who handles what touches him intimately, clothes and bedding, resists the move to follow him into his room and give him the goodnight kiss that a mother is entitled to, from childhood surely for all his life—the two men wouldn't be aware of this need. She herself does not know if she resists out of fear. Is there some sort of parenthesis in the mind: how can you fear your own child?

Neither Lyndsay nor Adrian plays any organised sport— Adrian likes to remark with pretended ruefulness, How can I

retire, as I don't play golf? A vision of an eternity as an endless stretch of greens, tees, sand pits, small flags. He's always
been a much diverted spectator of rugby, however, since he
played scrum half in student days; on Saturdays he plans to
pass the afternoon for his son, turning on the TV with the en-
quiring invitation glance to be joined in the livingroom.

The form of exercise Adrian and Lyndsay take is long
walks, ordinarily they would go off into the bush somewhere
at least once a month, spend a weekend at some small resort
from which they could cover trails with the exuberant dog,
its sense of freedom matched by theirs. Paul knows, come
Saturday-Sunday they would be doing what leisure best meant
to them, and besides was essential for healthy people getting
older. Living with a small child of his own two generations
removed, he's been used to thinking of them as old, but in
these days close in this house, a way one or the other moved,
a reaction between them, a gesture or turn of phrase either
used, returned them from individuals to what they had been
before. Parents. He can't tell them, as he wishes, that they
could go off and enjoy their walk in the country, he knows
from living with Benni how, never mind the exercise, you
have the need to do some things together, surely even in a
marriage as long as theirs . . . how long must it be? . . . doesn't
remember. He'll be all right. He's learning to be alone in his
new way just as he and his sisters learnt in the old way when
parents were absent from this house. But he can't raise the
subject because logic of this kind brings up the unimaginable
state: why is he here with them, at all. Adrian and Lyndsay,
parents who are now also the new devout missionaries, no
care possible for self, in this private place of asylum, taking
care of the lit-up leper.

Nadine Gordimer

Most evenings the three listen to music. Adrian has a re-
markable collection, not only CDs but rare LPs, even 78s, and
the gamut of equipment, antique and the latest, to play them.
Adrian has to go about the house to find the particular recordings he wants Paul and Lyndsay to enjoy—an early Klem-
perer, a contemporary Barenboim—since the racks that hold
his collection are stacked here and there, even in passages.
Equipment to provide occupation in retirement (he'd been
promising himself for years to find time to catalogue his
treasures properly), they had had to clear from what was to
be his study become the son's refuge. Of course Paul knows
he is welcome to banish the listening silence during the
weekday desertion by parents (that is how Adrian and Lyndsay think of their absence at office and Chambers). Sometimes he tries it, the complete *Fidelio* an experiment, and if
the recording is a single human voice, Callas with the systole
and diastole of the breath that empowers it, present within
his four walls, it is one-half of a dialogue with what is missing in his present. Full orchestral stuff which perhaps Adrian
hopes for his son will be a rousing affirmation of being, is an
unwelcome crowd gate-crashing the silence. He'd rather strain,
half-consciously alert to make out if maybe there might be
the small domestic sounds of Primrose moving about in the
kitchen.

His sister Jacqueline lives with an accountant husband in
another suburb. She was a Montessori nursery-school teacher
and has substituted their own two children for the general
brood who used to receive her maternal care. She sends her
brother home-made concoctions she remembers or thinks he
likes. Pork sausage rolls. Once a baked banana pudding, up-
graded, the accompanying note says, 'from the treat we used

to love, by a good slosh of brandy'. She brings the offerings to the gate and Primrose takes delivery. The first occasion, he went to greet his sister beyond the bars and she began to cry at the sight of him; so he kept himself out of the way, after that. But then he had gone strangely, slowly, back to the house and to the bathroom to see in the mirror what she saw. He had become thinner; but it seemed to him only that he looked falsely innocent, artificially younger than he remembered his face as he shaved—before.

Susan, the sister married to an ostrich farmer become unexpectedly prosperous due to the worldwide demand for low-cholesterol steaks, doesn't know what to say to him and phones their mother to enquire after his progress. She graduated from art school but with the inherited rigorous standards of her ambitious mother transferred from a professional vocation to that of art, saw that she did not have the talent to become an abstract painter or a postmodernist, a conceptualist, of originality, and with her father's adaptation to circumstances worked as a restorer of museum paintings before taking to her farmer and his surrealist birds. Emma, the biological prank sister who followed her brother's birth so precipitately, lives in South America, where she is foreign correspondent for a British newspaper. The emigration came about, as it does for many females, because she had married a foreigner—a Brazilian lawyer met when her mother invited him home to dinner during a conference on constitutional law he was attending in South Africa. This daughter was a precocious divorcée, a law student at the time; the only one of the siblings following any tradition of parental careers. Emma's emails greet *my almost-twin* (only twelve months between their births) *hardly popped out before papa popped me in* and they arrive every few days to that room designated for him, the very beep of the computer a kind of lively grimace, from her, at what had—what was the term—befallen him. She had no embarrassed reverential awe, no disguised distaste for how he must find himself as one could never imagine oneself being; she asked, came right out with it: *absolutely ghastly, I try to imagine how you cope, it must be so unreal, I think it's a good thing I'm far away because I wouldn't believe it, some sci-fi thing in you, my boetie, I'd just hug you. Can't accept you've winged down giving off rays from horrible Outer Space. Lowest common denominator in corny entertainment. Ugh. We'd have a good laugh together, as we've done since we burbled as babies. The sheer absurdity of all this, in your life. Crazy. D'you mean you can't even have a fuck?* There isn't anything she can't say, at her distance—she keeps that distance by not calling, and he understands; she somehow knows he has nothing to relate. Sometimes he sends a brief email in reply, she knows the formula is all he can 'manage', *good to hear from you, got the hug, love ya.* If she tears the band-aids of convention off his state, it's a wild release; for the moments while he reads and falls to the temptation to reread, he hears himself laughing out loud. But it won't work to leave himself raw, like this, management exists only in ordinariness being imposed, applied and maintained as long—long as he lasts. A test-decreed end. Or test-decreed survival. No more emanation, no light.

He wanders the rooms of the house as if idly cataloguing objects recognised and things acquired, added, for which there is no memory embedded, representing periods and desires of two people postdating the time he quit this house where he is returned as emanation. Inanimate things do not receive cognisance of an ectoplasm, only living beings are aware of such a presence. The Labrador taking a stolen siesta on a sofa lifts her head at someone there, in the room.

Through the deep windows of the livingroom, legs thrown over the sill, he finds himself in the garden.

It's only at what must be some regularly spaced day that the man with the great fork or spade or shears is there: the salute. It has become a wave of an implement waggled in the air. He's tried to call back an opening for some exchange but the few words composed in Zulu are not responded to except for a grin that might or might not be incomprehension, maybe the grammatical construction is laughable or the man speaks another language. There's his own voice answered, by a raucous bird-cry. The hadedas come from the rooftop and thrust their telescope beaks sounding for worms in the lawn, as if he were not there.

Seven- (could it be as young as that) eight-year-old with a catapult made from a jacaranda branch and some strips of rubber (old bicycle tyre) aims at the doves still mourning their recitative up on the gutters. The game is forbidden and the one time a bird is hit and falls limp but with life in the glint of the eye it's understood why: death is forbidden. What happened to the bird. Concealed in a dustbin. No, secrecy has more imagination than that, more than the lawmakers could credit. It was buried, a playmate brought in for the rites, there behind the old compost heap, with the stems of some daisies stuck upright in the soil.

It's not often a grown man lies down on his back on grass; there're the plastic-thonged chaises longues meant to be unfolded in the sun or under the shade of the jacaranda. To a naked upturned face; no sky; space. No cloud to give scale in the bleach of glare, no blue to give depth. Grass stirs beneath with minute scratching claws. Perhaps there are beetles, ants, moving unseen as the predator cells in their terrain, all life is one, it's said. On this crawling sensation some weight thuds down, it's the playmate, there's a giggling, gasping struggle; if it's the playmate in turn thrust low on the irritation of the grass, ends in tears. Comes the liar's appeal for mercy—There's a *gogga* biting me! So this grass is the referee in the savage small-boy fights that are also forbidden. *Is that how you treat friends? It's not a game. You will hurt each other.*

Which is exactly the intention. To make the cry-baby resort to the intervention of nature to save him from defeat, while the victor never calls for help as *he* lies pinned to the grass beneath him. Adults put a stop to the battles; or did the atavism pass, had its stage, along with thumb-sucking, and only the white-flag appeal, there's a *gogga* biting me, become part of the family vocabulary to call for the mercy of laughter when you found yourself in a tight spot.

Dust off the loose grass. Getting to the feet still creates disorientation, this wears off here in the garden, where it's usual to stroll slowly unless one is a boy racing to catch a ball. A rose responds to closeness with faint scent. Lilies: slugs, snails, suck the thick, sculptured stems, some years in the pest cycle. In reconciliation—maybe—with the playmate, there is taken up an adult offer of a cent for each snail gathered. To squash them was messy and they were dropped to die in a pail of water. Hot? A snail is not a bird. There's a ceiling at which compassion begins, lowly creatures are below it. That's the innocence that remains unchanged in a garden.

The ring from the house is Berenice's second call of the day. Excitement in her voice, her vocabulary a genre she's speaking from, she's just received confirmation of the big deal, a contract that includes all television, radio, Internet rights as well as newsprint, with clients who've closed their account with a sky-high-profile rival agency and come to her stable. He is aware this exaltation is also relief because her commission on such a deal will be substantial enough to help pay laboratories and doctors.

—And you?— A different voice, the cadence of the unspoken between them. He can tell her there's an email from Emma.

—Oh Emma's great! Read it to me?—no, when I come this afternoon.—

At what is designated his lunchtime, Primrose has left a salad and fresh bread set out, coffee on the electric hot tray, there's a call from his mother, but the preoccupation in that voice is different. She has lost a case, judgment given against her client. She does not bother him with the telling of it. He would only feel he must commiserate. Why should he. The judgment on him, from whom, who knows where, has no recourse; there will be an application for right to appeal, on behalf of the client.

It is Agency style that clients at once address even senior personnel by the first name; the unspoken premise is that the client and the professional who is designing promotion of what the client wants to sell are in partnership rather than the calculated relation of hire and pay. Berenice: this one has a manner of treating the client as an equal in the flair, the style of campaign she is planning, no matter how obvious it is that the client has no such faculties of his or her own. This 'Berenice' somehow conveys assurance that the campaign is an inside job, she's part of the client's company advancing itself. Her smart asides on public taste, and endearing swift movements indicting her own, her small pauses, notation in the brand jingle of advertising-agency-client dialogue, to mark sensitive understanding when the client wavers a doubt . . . All these that had come to her spontaneously now seemed a professional technique. It could be produced while the one to whom her real responses should be directed was shut away, not only in some physical place, but from any part in the daily, nightly existence of herself and the child. The child: as if the child and the life that he represented were all that there had been in the complex one of a man and a woman? Responses cut and dangling. How could it take an illness to do this? That's all, just an illness. She had not needed, while jesting or expertly elaborating on serious matters appealing to the shrewdness of clients, to think of him when he was off in his wilderness, passionate as he was to be there; she somehow could not, in need now, summon ability to think of him as he was in the room made a confinement in the house of occasional family gatherings. Even his voice on the telephone, what did it convey of where he was, what he was. Even the afternoon visits in that other wilderness between them, his childhood garden, where the tension in him at the pain of her being there and not there for him made her feel she was in control of another's mind, not herself, in another time.

She hears herself convincing sceptical clients with enthusiastic voice, fan-spread hands winking magenta fingernails, bracelets sliding back on rather beautiful forearms, of the intelligence of her plan of action. From the most dourly resistant of them she drew admiration to be read in the relaxation of face muscles although they continued to let their sidekicks do the questioning. In-house, between consultations with clients, there was the usual bantering and exchange of private views on their idiosyncrasies—Agency gossip with colleagues, several of whom were black, now, in the Agency's policy of self-interest showing conformation to Affirmative Action (some clients came from new black-owned companies), young women indistinguishable in their styles of dress and vocational jargon, except for the colour of their skin and elaborate arrangements of their hair. Only a select few of her colleagues knew the details of what had happened to that rather dishy man of hers who was always off in the bush saving the planet. Disaster is private, in its way, as love is. Other people will be pruriently curious (love-matters) or trivialise with their syrup of sympathy (matters of disaster).

Her professional persona, carrying on for her. That had to be. She drank champagne someone brought in to celebrate the triumphant contract, quipped and laughed in shared pride. She went out often to dinner with special friends among the colleagues, usually white, as had been before the Affirmative Action ones had arrived—those seemed to have better things to do with their leisure. At dinner, as always, everyone 'talked shop' and it was quite usual for someone to come without their other-occupied lover or spouse. Mutual friends, Paul's and hers—difficult to explain to them, no offence meant—she became inclined to avoid. They wanted to talk about him, were concerned to know how she really felt, sought her acceptance of their support for that which was not clear—was it because her husband and their dear friend was likely sentenced to death, or was it for the unimaginable state of her isolation from him, parting while he was still alive, somewhere. Should they call him? Could she take books, documentaries and comedies they'd recorded, letters, to him? If she did deliver whatever they remembered to give her, they did not receive any response to let them know that their gifts of friendship and thought for him meant anything. Perhaps he was too weak to respond, though they'd been given to understand he was recuperating while still an Untouchable—radiation coming from his body. Or was it that the state of being taboo to others produced exactly the complementary within the isolated one: ability to communicate stifled.

Most unfortunate it was decided that the grandparents
with whom little Nickie got along so happily, perhaps should
have no contact with him, though the doctors had been vague
about whether secondhand proximity to emanation was any
danger; Lyndsay went to Chambers and Adrian mixed with
fellow board members. Yet certainly a wise precaution, no
matter how remote the shaft of invisible light might be, for
the grandmother not to be in the proximity of the child since
she was the one who touched what had been against the lit-
up body, clothes, sheets, the utensils that came from contact
with lips and tongue. Lyndsay and Adrian tactfully left the
couple alone in the garden if they happened to be home
when Benni visited. But they felt that Paul's wife and themselves must have some private meaning for one another and
this should find expression in some gesture beyond telephone
exchanges. In association between Adrian and Benni, the danger would seem so remote a risk; Paul was no longer too weak
to bath alone, his father did not have to expose himself by
helping him. Adrian followed the impulse to call Benni at her
Agency, with a suggestion. And so Berenice's secretary transferred a call from the father-in-law asking how Berenice
would feel about coming out to dinner with him—would she
think it all right, for her? Of course, he didn't say, you'd be
going home to the child. Apparently she dismissed this as no
risk. Fine, I'd like to.

Adrian must have given some consideration about where
to go. He was a sensitive man who loved and appreciated
women and had always chosen for a woman the kind of restaurant where she would feel and look her best, her sort of place,
no matter how strange the occasion might be. When he began to be drawn with such finality to Lyndsay he had ended

a dwindling love affair, outworn on both sides, over a meal in a restaurant that the woman favoured, and he had chosen for his first meal with Lyndsay the restaurant he felt he knew instinctively would be the setting for her to begin her place in his life, for life.

This young woman his son had chosen.

The restaurant was not one of those where family celebrations were held because they were familiar to the parents— good food and wine list to be counted on. It was in a suburb where white civil servants, mainly Afrikaners, had lived neatly around their Apostolic and Dutch Reformed churches, and had been deserted by them when after their regime had been defeated, black people had the right to move in as neighbours. Then it had become a place where all that had been clandestine, the mixing of blacks and whites, not necessarily the political activists who had won that freedom, was open. People in television, the theatre, advertising, journalists, and all the hangers-on of the arts and crafts, made it fashionable among themselves. An alternative to corporate chic, which they couldn't have afforded anyway. And in addition to rap and jazz bars and restaurants which gays or blacks favoured like clubs, vegetarians could find dishes to conform to different versions of their faith, mixed-race lovers were not something exotic confined to the new black upper class and their white partners patronising elegant enclaves of the old white rich. And there was something the corporate rich hadn't thought of as part of night life, a bookshop that stayed open very late.

Yes of course, this was one of the restaurants she'd been to customarily, with Agency pals and sometimes with Paul. The quarter was lively, scents of herb shops, marijuana, spicy cooking drifted into the streets along with wafts of music. Paul had found treasures of old books, scuffed and rat-nibbled early accounts of pre-white-settled terrain, river courses, and information on pre-industrial climate, in the bookshop's secondhand bins.

His father had chosen what he thought would be her kind of place. She wanted to respond to this wish to please, to divert—and—was it—console both the father and herself by breaking bread, drinking wine in a covenant of those invisible liens that must exist, unthought-of, unrecognised in the Christmas pecks on the cheek, between the one who generated, from his body, the son, and the one who receives the son in hers. Presence of death standing by makes a sacrament of tenuous relationships. They talked quite animatedly. He smilingly half-confessed his choice of the restaurant. —Thank you for the pretext that's brought us here! Never tried Melville before. I don't know about Lyn, she might have, with some young legal colleague. I think she'd like it anyway, we must come and have a meal. What good and imaginative food.—

He was interested in the ethics of advertising, how did the industry expect to make up, for instance, for the loss of exposure it could offer now that beer promotion for the huge sports-events market was banned by the government: this must be a headache for the agencies? He was not afraid, either, of bringing up matters which assumed, as present, opinions of the quarantined. What kind of school did she and his son think of for their son, only a baby still, but he supposes a changed country both made a 'normal' education possible as it never was under segregation when Paul was a child, and raised new questions of choice, nevertheless. No segregation, black and white; but boys' school or co-ed?

The pleasant warmth of people her own age and kind around her, the food and wine to her taste; it was the element lapping about someone other than herself, as she talked, she contributed to an exchange with the well-informed and attentive man opposite her—the son closely resembled the mother, this man could be taken without any other recognition, for himself, and whatever hidden self might be. She heard her own voice speak, a professional facility. She ate without distinguishing one flavour or consistency from another. The wine stirred someone else's blood, not hers. She, so naturally sociable, called to in greeting of lifted glasses from other tables, where fellow habitués happened to be, endured in desperation—surrounded by—the alien presence that was other people.

In her call next morning she was telling the son what a good time she had.

Why? So that he wouldn't worry about her. So that he wouldn't be saddened by the thought that she could enjoy herself without him? Perhaps forever. Her own behaviour most of the time is an enigma to her. Had she ever found the atmosphere in that place her native element; yet this must have been evident in her, else why would a man like his father—no, *Adrian*, a man revealed as one of sensibility—have known it would be the place to take her to outside the anonymity of past family treats.

Paul. Often silent, when they were there partying with her colleagues? Just thoughtfully listening or, she would think, his head full of those vast contradictory factors in his beloved wilderness just left. Paul with her and not present. Cosmic problems. Another 'why'; why must her man take on the survival of the whole bloody world, and now himself a threatened species.

Calls cut off more than the telephonic connection through wires glittering in the air, cabled underground, bounced from satellites, when the receiver goes silent and is put down.

How's today? You up and about . . . I'll fetch you at ten-thirty tomorrow, time enough, don't you think, traffic's not heavy then. Lyndsay. The event is the occasion of tests at a laboratory.

I'm furious, as you can hear, darling—some bloody client's complaining about a TV slot, the handsome guy lounging on the new state-of-the-art sports car looks too much like a queen, I have to meet our offended corporate late this afternoon. But I'll come early before I go to work tomorrow. Berenice/Benni. We'll be with the early birds in the garden.

There is even a call on a mobile from Derek who is driving back to the city from reconnaissance of the proposed pebble-bed nuclear site. His findings so far are a bit too complex to go into on the phone while driving, he'll rough out a report and get it over to Benni. Derek does not want to risk breaching the quarantine in any way, does not really trust proximity in the fresh air of No-Man's-Land. And this is all right, quite understood, Derek has kids, you know. The mobile doesn't wait for the conclusion of Derek's apologies, cuts off into the ether between one syllable and the next.

The disappearances of these disembodied callers leave the room a vacuum at the same time filling up with the overwhelming furtive sounds, even when inert stretched on the bed or standing there, in the middle of staring emptiness, of himself: the breathing, fingers stirring in the current of blood as hands hang from wrists, odour of himself distilled by days and nights here undiluted by contact with the bodies, with the essence of others. Lyndsay is quickly in and out as she makes the bed. The old dog the parents think of as at least some sort of companion has come in only once, twitched its flared nose along the hospital hold-all which it rejected on the day of arrival, turned from it again.

Go out and play.

For the first few moments there, eyelids alternately squeezing and lifting wide at the immersion in that benign illumination, of the sun, birds who ring out like mobile phones. But there is no connection to be made between wild creatures, even the half-domesticated frequenters of the suburbs feeding on cultivated flowers, lawn worms, compost bugs, and the summons of technology. Telephone ring. In the bush in the forest among the dunes the mangroves the swamps, the creatures ignore you. Devices that regulate your being have nothing to do with theirs—unless they are hunted, expelled from their places in the universe—yes, air habitat as well as land—by logging, burning off, urban, industrial and rural pollution. Radiant nuclear fallout.

No connection between that quarantine room and out here.

The garden. It's both the place banished to in order to be got rid of by the preoccupations of an adult house, and the place to be yourself, against orders. Homework abandoned unfinished, there's no reproach in the nagging cries of hadedas, as they touch down on trees and earth-beds, close by.

Could almost put out a hand and touch one. The mother-of-pearl sheen casually attractingly flashed as the dull dark plumage catches the sun; wouldn't have noticed then just as it was years too soon for the glint of a glance from a woman to be caught.

The bits of wood from the greengrocer's fruit boxes, begged off Mr Farinha in his corner shop. Bright nails. Saw from the garden shed and hammer from the domestic repairs cupboard where spare lightbulbs and torch batteries were jumbled (other fathers are better-organised handymen). They can be arranged as they were, patterned about the open lawn, the glittering nails, and wheels from an old lawn-mower— old baby-stroller, could be. The boxcart into which this stuff set out is transformed, twisting unsteadily down the paths over there and clattering through the yard (concrete surface then) where Primrose is distantly singing a comfortingly monotonous work-song to herself.

Nothing outside doors and walls is ever really tamed. Confined. Roots of a pepper tree (*Schinus molle*) humping up under concrete once had to be dug up, severed. This boys' wilderness for tussling contests and cricket runs toted with a stick on sand, the breathless heat of sin in experiment with mutual masturbation down in the neglected patch behind the high, overgrown pampas grass, opened out into what cannot be reached lying in the designated room or sitting alone with plenty of reading matter in the livingroom it is better not to frequent too much. Here, radiance goes dark inside the body's terrain, there's only the light of the sun on the skin, rosy through eyelids closed at rest, not in sleep. The wetlands of St Lucia walked—how many months ago?—there are two Eras, BR, before discovery of the gland gone malignant, and AR, after radiance—that wilderness can be walked again from this small one, sequence by sequence, impression by impression, scent by scent. Alert as you go, you only register, with perhaps some moments of analysis, what there is to be understood later. The reading matter has not included the report passed on by Benni; it has been lying at the foot of the bed as if it were some irrelevant unsolicited leaflet, a piece of professional junk mail. Not to be allowed to distract from whatever it is that somehow totally occupies such concentration as there is. Survival, probably. While here with eyes climbing favoured trees, moving over the exhilarated pace of somersaults, pursuing the capture of a vivid grass snake green under kicked-aside leaves, he could think of looking at conclusions gathered from someone else's walk in the wilderness of swamp, mangrove, watery broth of life.

But when he got himself roused, back into quarantine to pick up the few sheets of paper conscientiously word-processed by an institute secretary, he put the thing aside, not on the foot of the bed again but slid on a pile of video cassettes.

Only out there, the garden, could the wilderness be gained, the unfinished homework be escaped. Leg over the sill; lying on the grass the many hours not tallied with a stick tracing in the sand. The days.

Nights. The nuclear family, father mother son, is asleep in reconstitution, reduced by quarantine.

One night, the dog barked frantically in the small hours and Lyndsay got up to follow as it plunged released through the front door into the driveway. In the arrested silence between night and day the interruption of the dog echoed from a hard black sky. The security light triggered by any movement within its orbit caught a man spot-lit like a celebrity, approaching. She shouted, What do you want! Response customary for mendicants, panhandlers, idiotic for an invader with what was the shape of a weapon of some sort in the hand clutched at his side. The dog danced and leapt, barking deafeningly but the man must have heard her anyway and she heard, as if they were yelling in mad conversation, his curses at her in an African language and the foulest scatological English, as he stood his ground a moment before twisting violently to race ahead of the dog and half-scramble, half-vault over the garden's iron-bar gate.

The son down the passage, doubly isolated by the soporific prescribed for him, and the husband asleep on the side of his good ear with only the other, increasingly less reliable, above the bedclothes, were not roused; the son on a remote level of consciousness and the husband, hearing at reduced volume the kind of annoying fuss of the dog that generally had no cause other than its bad dreams.

In the morning when she told the two of the man in the driveway, they were amazed, reproachful in concern. But why didn't you call one of us! Two men in the house, why does a woman go to face an intruder in the middle of the night! Adrian knows this woman, his, is courageous in everything she does, but . . .

My dear mama, foolhardy, I won't say stupid! Her son.

She pulled a smiling, deprecating mouth at the concern and the reproach.

Adrian. His father didn't seem to feel it as any diminution of manhood, that incident. You don't have to be macho—the quick word of judgment by which Benni measures male reactions so evident, she relates, in her working milieu—simply to accept that there are some situations which by reason of physique if nothing else, a male is the one fit to deal with. Adrian seemed concerned only to assure himself that Lyndsay was unharmed in any way at all, by the existence of a threat, by an experience of fear, as if he wanted to go over reverently that face that body that spirit of hers to be certain the five-minute confrontation in the night hadn't been traumatic: changed everything in her. You don't ever think, none of your business, in the ordinary course of living your own adult life, that there still may be this kind of sexually-charged emotion in your father for a woman, the woman that is your mother.

His father, having hired a permanent night watchman equipped with intercommunication to a security patrol company, has filed the incident, dealt with appropriately, among present living conditions.

It depends whose. An incident without harmful consequences may have another consequence within another living condition. A young man wouldn't have slept through the obvious summons of commotion if he were not less than a man, less than himself, stoned out of his mind into impotence as an inability to take any action, by drugs swallowed and radiance through the circulation of arteries blinding the brain. This's the monologue when lying in the quarantine's four walls while they, the others, Benni/Berenice, Adrian, Lyndsay, the friends who use the safe-distance telephone and email to enquire how you're doing, are all what is known as about their daily business. Busy-ness.

The garden is where the company of jacaranda fronds finger the same breeze that brushed the boy's soft cheek, where caught in peripheral vision a cent's-worth of never-exterminated snail moves by peristalsis over a stone, there is the wise presence that changes solitude of monologue into some kind of dialogue. A dialogue with questions; or answers never sought, heard, in the elsewhere. Not even the wilderness, where they must have, sometime, disturbed the readings of surveying instruments; the body of a fish floating belly-up? The doctors say there is significant improvement in those other readings. The radiance will soon fade and cease completely and the twenty-first-century leper may go back to touch and be touched.

Accepted and accepting.

What is it to go back to. You'll soon be home, had enough of us! Lyndsay's delight, for him. Berenice, across the space of No-Man's-Land—Why shouldn't we go off on a little trip, then? Indulge ourselves, one of the exclusive resorts the Agency represents, these really great game reserves ... no ... you've had enough of being away, just us and Nickie in our own place.

What is it: to go back.

The individual, the woman, the desire—the persona Benni/Berenice. Create her as the father did the mother, going over her being after she'd endangered it shouting, *What do you want.*

The man standing alone in the night of the garden ran away, back. The only time out in the garden ever at that time of night was when allowed to stay up to celebrate a New Year in a radiance of fireworks.

Back, to gain forgiveness, make up to the small boy (he's the spitting image of you over again) for desertion by *Daddy! Paul!* while the fingers had to be prized off the bars of the gate. Oh the boy's so young, that will be forgotten, filed away in childhood.

Only to come back, maybe, before a psychiatrist trying to unknot an adolescent's painful aggression. So many half-grown about whom no parents can fathom why these menacing creatures they've produced are as they are.

What do you want. What did you want. What did you settle for.

Five years passed—a state of existence in which the question—if it is one, because a choice was made—doesn't sound from within. There was—is—no place for it there. But *this* unimaginable concept of Life Time, the inconceivable: a state of existence which could-should never have happened, brings a knowing of that which was not admitted. The emanation irradiates the hidden or undiscovered.

To go back, to the contradiction that surely cut through the intimacy a man and a woman make together. That unit of being that is sexual fulfilment within the other conditions of being, *being in the world*, commitment of religious or political faith, commitment of values (can't weigh them in year-end bonus), what you live by in what matters, idea of what is meaningful for each in the aims of work, beyond the common needs it meets—can it be divided. You go your way I go mine while we belong easily together. A good fit. The evidence of that achievement the two-in-one tender flesh of the child. Who wants to face the fact that this 'achievement' also can result from the greatest possible alienation between a man and a woman 'together': rape.

Benni means well when Berenice offers a weekend transition from the state where the Untouchable has been a hermit within his own body—my god, of course she's tried to understand what this is, in her way—and coming: home. To take up where everything was left off. Meant well. So why allow an answer to a question, so long never put to the self, to open up such significance. It was nothing, her thought to please, quickly passed over. A nothing he has all the time in this existence to follow how and why it would come to mind in the one who proposed it. For Benni there is a Berenice solution to his return from an absence unlike any, a few days' break in the bush offered by one of the clients whose public relations the Agency handles. Luxury suites, pool and sauna, the Big Five sure to be seen on game drives, a portable bar on board the open-viewing vehicle. He loves the bush doesn't he, its animals, birds, insects, before he goes home again to their threesome life together let him return to make the connection with the working life he's so wrapped up in. For Benni, Berenice's recommendation is a microcosm of that wilderness. She's right, in a way. These places simulate life in the wild for indigenous animals who otherwise would not survive industrial and urban expansion; the territory bought by what is known as the leisure industry is land where the equally indigenous people were driven out by conquest of old colonial wars and exchanges of papers of possession for paper money, ever since, between generations of conquerors become lawmakers. Many of the corporate clients of whom the Agency is proud (high-profile is the coveted category in the business) are consortia that bid for rights to build resorts where the environment won't survive this kind of development, nevertheless. There was—is, he must not think of as no longer there, the terrain where he is not—a consortium lobbying the government with assurance of exceptional tourist potential, economic uplift of the surrounding region (the full litany), for such a scheme to build an hotel, casino, yacht marina as part of the vast drainage plan the government envisages. Development Disaster.

Whom does Berenice believe. Him, her man, or the client. What is her conviction when he comes from the wilderness and tells of the irreplaceable forest felled to make way for the casino, the fish floating belly-up in all that's left of a watercourse diverted to feed an Olympic-size swimming pool and replica of one of the fountains of Rome. What's her conviction within herself. His, or the client's? Or it's not as crude as that. Macho as that, she would interpret. It's something— Stop. Stop hearing the answer. But you cannot go back without knowing it.

She is that persona who has no need of convictions.

What is it? A terrible lack. A kind of awful purity? A virginity; or underdevelopment. That term fits.

Don't judge. For five years, if you count only the outward symbol of marriage as the unit of intimacy, not the love affair that preceded the formality, there was present always that while occupying the same bed you don't occupy the same fundament: to know your conviction of *being in the world.* Conviction, which? You cannot have two to live tolerantly by, outside the sense of self. One for the client and one at home. How could he, himself, whose work, reason-to-be is preserving life, live so long with an intimate, herself, who was successfully complicit in destroying it.

Living in isolation, all along. Even when inside the woman.

Later, in the garden, away from the closeted emanation in that room, what is this all about but an obvious matter of the incompatibility between the advertising industry and environmental protection. Two clichés. *So what?* Can't even call it by its true term. Irreconcilability. Because the world, in distinction from the individual, has no absolutes, there's a mix that goes along prescriptively with the mixed economy. And what about the woman, Benni/Berenice. What a prick the woman's chosen man has been. Yes, revealed as nothing but the prick in his relation to her.

The innocence of the tree that was climbed, the perspective of being alive, from up there, the mind's sketch of the treehouse-gynaeceum of the sisters—everything accepted, the sin behind the pampas grass, capture of the freedom of butterflies, fall of the slingshot bird.

But it was in the Garden that expulsion came once there was Knowledge.

Divorce? Divorce after she's endured, on her side of the quarantine, did her job, earned the means of common needs, took care of the child calling *Daddy Paul*, smiled and joked anecdotally for normality across the divide between outdoor chairs. While this brings no counsel from the uncertain waverings of the jacaranda fronds, tongues in trees, there comes a prolonged ringing from the house. Goes ignored, until whoever it was hangs up. But the caller determinedly keeps trying. Such obstinacy must somehow be responded to. Still— as now—unsteady, upright from supine, the way to the house seems slowly gained. The ringing gives up; and starts once more, an encouragement.

—So you laz-zy, how's it? Chief, *haai!* We never hear from you! So much happening. I'm back onto the pebble-bed scene, now, it's dynamite, my man, I can tell you. But what are the doctors doing, keeping you locked away like this, do you feel okay? When're you coming back? Aren't you due for remittance of sentence by now . . . So . . . good, that's great. Sharp—sharp! Say, you hear the latest—the Institution of Nuclear Engineers says the new reactor at Koeberg gonna be 'walk away safe'. 'Walk away safe.' I thought you'd like to take that walk, Bra. But if the Minister gives Government go-ahead, we'll have him in court against this 'favourable environmental impact assessment evaluation' his boys have come up with. Man, I've got plenty to tell you, what's going on, we're getting more support groups joining protest every day. Big names. Amazing. I promise you. The man's gonna find the nuclear a hot seat . . . so when can I come to your place, I don't know where you are—

—Not a good idea for you, I want to see you, Bra, but we can't sit in the same room, we'd be in the garden like a couple of kids sent out of the way. And even then, who knows. Why should you risk anything at all, I'm my own experimental pebble-bed nuclear reactor.—

Laughter bursting into the receiver. —Sharp! Sharp! But nonsense, *non-sense*. What about the weekend. I'll be back in town. What's the address? I'll turn up in the afternoon and bring you some stuff to work over. We need you.—

When he arrives he has to be backed away from as he throws out his arms for the African shoulder-hug that's come out of the expression of freedom fought for together among black men and has done away with the inhibition of whites that God-fearing heterosexual males don't embrace. (Thapelo at seventeen was in a Mkhonto we Sizwe cadre, another kind of combat in the bush.)

How can you manage what you are, to others. Primrose, her statement to stay on in the risk of quarantine when the right thing was for the parents—and the leper himself—to insist that the faithful retainer be treated like anyone else outside the responsibility of progenitors, and be sent beyond harm. What is the threshold of risk to be decreed for different people—what about the paper plates touched by radiant saliva on spoons and forks, got rid of. Thrown away in the trash to lie on waste dumps picked over by kids from black squatter camps. What is 'rid of' in terms of any pollution, it's a life's work to inform us that it's not only what is cast into the sea that comes back to foul another shore, no matter whose it is.

This man is not that barely-literate woman; he's scientifically literate, awareness of the insidious power of radiation is in his daily field. Primrose does not believe in what she cannot see; he knows what is not to be seen as it exudes from one who is his Chernobyl, his own Koeberg experimental nuclear reactor. How was it these two had no fear; too easy to attribute this sentimentally, as a white man descended from a history posited on the tenet that blacks were worse, to evidence that both were blacks, and better. Willing to take risks, in contact with fellow humans. More likely, for this ex–Freedom Fighter colleague in scientific research as for the uneducated woman, he's been exposed and accustomed to many threats in childhood in the quarantine of segregation, before those of war.

Thapelo brought cold beer and a field briefcase tight with documents. Beer in the garden was the first drink after decreed abstinence. Worth taking the risk of reaction, in the company of a workmate. The sun drowned under the horizon of shrubs and the garden darkened, until a light appeared on the terrace and the mother's voice called affectionately, a familiar coaxing echo, Paul don't you think it's time you came in.

ii / *States of Existence*

She pulled a smiling, deprecating mouth at the concern and the reproach.

If someone had to get shot by an intruder it mustn't be one of her beloved men; only now come to know, through another kind of threat, the urgency of that love. Couldn't tell them. That was her reason to be out before the intruder, alone. A threat you could counter. But that much was clear in all that was confused in what had happened to them; Paul, Adrian, Lyndsay. To try and make sense of it there were devices of different approach; she must place herself among these less subjectively, as a woman called 'Lyndsay'. Set it out. The meteor of the inconceivable fell upon the son; he was the one who became invisibly alight. Paul. What happened to him was not to be presumptuously compared with what happened within his radius to the father, Adrian, and the mother, Lyndsay. In yourself as progenitor you have somewhere a

stowed disaster kit, resourced both practically and psycholog-
ically to deal with a known list of existential crises in your
children's lives: career failure, suicidal loss of confidence,
doomed love affair, broken marriage, change of sexual orien-
tation, drug addiction, debt. They've had the broken marriage syndrome with the daughter born too soon after the
son, but it has proved to be a kick start for her rather than a
trauma, she has a new country, a new language and a new
man to fulfil her apparent needs. As a lawyer, in her early career the Lyndsay persona was familiar with the entire conventional list, but for years her career has been as a civil
rights and constitutional lawyer. Adrian proved to be the one
best in understanding of the way Emma could emerge from
the tangle of the early marriage; lawyer Lyndsay could simply provide the practical means to end the contract. He suggested to their daughter that you can perhaps destroy out of
pride and anger, too hastily, what may be essential for you.
She had been so crazily in love with the man, whatever had
happened to them since. Give yourself time to be sure whether
the heady power of rejection—making a decision while you
are drunk with it, it's potent—hasn't taken from you the one
you really want, worth an acceptance of all the disillusion
come about. So the girl who had married too young didn't
take the quick and tidy divorce; unaccountably, in her
mother's view (wasn't the childish marriage a casualty before
the register was signed), she took half a year to test herself
and did not regret it, confiding to her father that it had been
a good thing: she would leave the marriage now in calm
certainty it was not vital, within her or the man. The father
didn't protest or pass judgment, apparently this was all right,

for him, too? The process had been fulfilled, justifying what-ever the outcome.

Hazards like these have recognisable courses of action, emotional readjustments, to follow, even if individuals re-sponding don't always do so in the same way. What has happened—that formulation implies the past, what is here now is a present that has no existence in the range of experi-ence provided for. Only the Japanese would understand, maybe; they have had to make 'ordinary' ('normal' is a word that can't be used on this subject) the presence of children born, generations after the light greater than a thousand suns, with a limb or some faculty of the brain missing.

Paul's confrontation with an unimaginable state of *self*. She sees it in his face, the awkwardness of his body as if he feels the body does not belong to him, when he speaks, his choice of words, of what there is that can be said among all that cannot. She is aware of the state as she makes his bed and as she stands at the chuntering machine unable to leave off watching his contaminated clothes somersaulting in water behind a round window, Primrose standing by. This is Prim-rose's domain, no matter how contemptibly role-confining that may sound. Lyndsay's presence in the backyard laundry cannot be *ordinary*.

The endless hours he seems to spend in the garden. No book, no radio. Imagine, an attempt to leave the state behind in this prison-home. No-one could conjure that. It's more than a physical and mental state of an individual; it's a disembodi-ment from the historical one of his life, told from infancy, boyhood, to manhood of sexuality, intelligence and intellect. It's a state of existence outside the continuity of his life.

The evidence of such a phenomenon before her every morning when she puts her head round the door to greet him as she leaves for Chambers and the structure of the law ready to deal with the dislocations of human existence on the Statute Book, the return to find him in the darkening garden or lying in his cell—this stirs unwanted recognition that there are other states of alienated existence.

Now also become unimaginable.

Fifteen years ago she sat in this house one night and said, I have to tell you something. The affair is over.

This same familiar room where their son sits with them in the relation of childhood, these nights, listening to music.

This room was where Adrian was told that his wife Lyndsay's four-year love affair with another man had ended. He was looking at her as he was to all those years later when she told him his son had a cancer of the thyroid gland; blue eyes black with intensity.

I thought you were going to tell me you were leaving.

She met the man at a conference through the advancement in her career he, Adrian, had made, in practicality, possible. For him love (one came at last to understand) is commitment to the fulfilment of the loved one. In their early life together he had taken on many responsibilities in the education of the children and distractions of domestic bothers, freeing her to continue her studies and pursue the right contacts to be admitted to the Bar, realise her ambition to become a civil rights lawyer. When she was briefed for a case that passionately interested her, her mood brought home was quickly matched by his; they would celebrate with her exposition of the issue for the layman he was, over their meal, late in bed. Sometimes she would say in reaction to his questions—a reflection on another's life—you could have been a very good lawyer, but he had wanted something else, also not realised, wanted to be an archaeologist. Go digging, as he dismissed the seriousness of the vocation become an avocation, subject of leisure reading and occasional viewings of the site of an archaeological find opened to the public. Not many become a Leakey or a Tobias. When they had to go for marriage, children and years might pass before, if ever, going digging could provide bread for a family, instead of studying for that profession he took, meantime, a junior position with prospects in a business firm, and indeed, with his wide intelligence that could not apply itself at less than its best, even to what did not really interest him, moved on to a successful middle-level niche in an international firm.

She became prominent enough in cases of civil rights to have worked with the great in the profession, Bizos and Chaskalson, in these final years of the old regime when daring legal opposition to it caught the attention of world support, while the powers of the world dilly-dallied whether or not to back, by sanctions against the regime, the liberation movement and its military action. She was invited here and there abroad to conferences on civil rights and constitutional law—this last in particular an aspect in which she was qualifying herself for the future: the country would have a new constitution, new laws to be upheld when the old regime was defeated.

It was at a conference in her home country, home city, in

which she was a member of the Bar Association's organising committee, that she met the man for the second time. He was a European in the sense that she was not; from Europe, fairly distinguished on the international legal conference circuit. Hospitable on home ground, she followed the protocol by which her local colleagues shared out the obligation to entertain the visitors. She invited this one, with whom at least she had previous acquaintance, to a dinner at this house. Adrian as host. The man was not the most outstanding personality round this table where one of the settings is now with paper plates, and it is not memorable whether he and the husband of the colleague, with whom he was conferring professionally for a second time, exchanged more than casual dinner-table remarks. In the usual enjoyable assessment of guests after they had gone—fascinating, boring, or about whom there was nothing much to say—no recall of mention of him. But that might be repressed memory.

Perhaps as a return for the hospitality in place of delivery of flowers, next day the man suggested they skip lunch-break refreshments provided at the conference centre and get something interesting to eat elsewhere. He was more amusing tête-à-tête than at a dinner table. Maybe he had been bored. A few days later they went for a drink she agreed was needed after a long conference session. The half-hour in a bar was a continued session of legal complexities discussed—he seemed to have a special respect for her knowledge of the law's constraints in this country of which he had no experience. When the conference closed and farewells were made he said his to her, last of all. So it was that moment among the crowd; suddenly there: they had to see one another again.

It could have been he who arranged to have her invited to

a seminar in his country. The laughter together, the shared ironies of the proceedings, the delighted discovery, each for each, of how the other's intelligent intuition worked, the sense of something new, in man-woman, waiting to be acknowledged, life beckoning, crooking a finger, led to a room in an hotel. Not the one where they were quartered along with their colleagues—they are not naïve adolescents—he might be seen leaving her room or she his at some hour open to only one interpretation.

How *girlishly* exciting it must have been. To be irresistibly attractive to a man: at forty-something, with a loving husband, grown children, a successful career in a male-dominated profession; moving into a new maturity of freedom. Not to be foregone; to be taken as the other chances had been, to become a civil rights lawyer, an Advocate with Chambers. Sexual freedom, oh yes. Not as an orthodox feminist, god forbid, totting up orgasms as a constitutional right, but as one who'd read Simone de Beauvoir and the time had come to remember her concept of 'contingent loves'. Sexual freedom, yes. But not only that. Freedom of something new in experience, association of this with another mind, personality, within the same shared structure of intellectual activity. Didn't have that already, the shared intellectual activity, in abundance with daily colleagues? But not in the special context of other intimacy!

Contingency requires that what the situation is contingent to be not displaced. A whole strategy has to be devised to ensure this, or at least attempt to. It implies a code of conduct—also ancillary to, distinct from the one that always has been followed in private and professional ethics. The invitations to conferences and seminars at the safe distance of abroad were the available means of taking the freedom of contingency while protecting what must not be affected by it; Adrian, the foundation Adrian-Lyndsay-son-and-daughters. Conferences that did not exist were just as good, for this purpose, as those that did. Surely there is a humane principle that lies save if not lives then the good order of life. That order was not materially deprived in any way: the code does not allow that. An advocate's earnings were sufficient to provide the usual contribution to school, university fees and family holidays, while paying for airfares to remote places where only urgent meetings of a non-professional kind were planned. The urgency was something come unbidden and undeniable, not to be self-questioned, too strong for that. As if some wilful drive that exists in everyone and can remain dormant, unevidenced, forever, an atavism not needed to be called upon, is suddenly, fiercely active.

She came home from these absences unlike any other and went back zestfully to the briefs awaiting at Chambers. (How was the last meeting—the Japanese, wasn't it . . . ? Australians. Oh nothing we don't already know.) She and Adrian made love in the compact of celebration of her being home. Wherever she had been in another persona. The lovemaking with the other had improved her own advances and responses. That is how unaccountable human relationships are. She saw that she pleasured Adrian as she believed she had not done quite so expertly before. That must be what some expert prostitutes—sex workers they're called now—acquire. Adrian must have attributed this to the deprivations of absence.

The man managed to get himself invited back to her country, her city, to teach a course of international jurisprudence at a university. They met in afternoons at motels in nearby small towns. His teaching programme was not onerous, he could have been spending hours in the library on private research in Roman Dutch Law as an attribute of colonialism he was known to be doing, on the spot, as it were. Her secretary at Chambers informed callers she was out at a meeting with a client. He encountered the husband and wife at gatherings in her colleagues' houses. It would have looked strange if he had never been invited, as he was on a previous visit, to their house; once again, he came to dinner among other guests. He noticed on a table in this livingroom where the old dog who is at least some company for the quarantined son now lies on a sofa, several tomes and coffee-table books on archaeology. And host Adrian noticed his casual interest, came up to talk to him. A pleasant exchange. Would you like to visit one of the sites? I could arrange for you ... Oh Cradle of Man and all that ... I should take advantage while I'm here—I must see if I can make some time, yes.

Of course he did not. Ordinary, unavoidable social intercourse is part of the code, one doesn't go beyond it.

But it was inevitable that what was contingent in the Seychelles or Bonn would come too close to be managed without error, a slip of vigilance in the familiar complacency provided by home. They were going to the theatre, the couple, and she had come back from a motel and left an open straw handbag tossed on their bed. Whether Adrian had some disquiet about her afternoon absences from Chambers lately whenever he happened to call her there, and looked in the bag (for an address, a name?)—bizarrely unlikely, either the suspicion or the act—or whether the plastic container that held the rubber diaphragm she wore against conception, familiar to him as part of her feminine paraphernalia in their bathroom cabinet, had fallen out of the bag, is not known. She never will know. Neither will she know how he got himself to open the thing and see it was empty. The device inside her.

So that was a whole new section and paragraph thereof to be added to the code.

He had said nothing when she came into their bedroom brushing her newly-washed red hair he always found so beautiful. They drove to the theatre, he seemed tired and they were comfortably quiet together. They chatted with acquaintances met in the foyer. During the performance she turned to whisper a remark to him and in the dark saw something that set her heart thudding out of rhythm with some sort of premonitory fear. A tear caught the light from the stage on his cheek screwed in anguish.

Anger battled with disbelief in the days, weeks that followed. And pain. Pain has to be managed. He asked, he demanded, who the man was. No-one you know. He guessed, was it—

No-one you know.

This one or that among her lawyer colleagues, their mutual friends—

No-one you know.

He did not accuse her, she did not defend herself; he did not give the ultimatum, end this or end us. He could not end Them, and she could not end Them.

He bore his pain and she bore his pain and anger.

The man went back where he came from. She continued for four years to go to conferences around the world. She was very successful in her profession. How was Adrian to know when there were conferences and when there were not. He was no part of the legal fraternity/sorority cognisant with such opportunities.

These are the facts.

Facts are what constitutes evidence; they do not go further than that.

I have to tell you something. The affair is over.

I thought you were going to tell me you were leaving.

Case closed.

Fifteen years lived since then. In closeness and warmth, unable to do without one another. Never, as the meaningful common phrase goes, looked at another man, and Adrian knew that. As for him—he is the swan who mates for life, he'd had his contingent loves before marriage; they were differently contingent, in the sense of to the real one that was coming. Only once there was an impulse to speak—say, forgive me; a moment of ill-advised weakness occasioned by some passing shakiness in the family, bringing the parents particularly close—one of the girls in trouble, wasn't ever the boy.

Perhaps he would have been amazed to be reminded, confronted, the eyes would have gone black with intensity, resounding the statement, I thought you were going to tell me you were leaving. And there they were living fifteen good years as if what she wanted forgiveness for, never was. Who had made that possible; he: having the inner strength to take the evidence: that his statement was refuted was a sign ordained, not to be questioned: they belonged to each other. Now the age of retirement coming—it's in that historical continuity of their life.

A state of existence. Unimaginable. Because her son, belonging to the historical continuity, brings a state of existence, his, before her days and nights, there returns a chapter not written, included, that surely cannot be believed was possible; could never happen to her as the son could not be thought ever to emanate danger out of the dark of his body.

Forget so much, what a blessing the electronic notebook gadget when listening to long-winded witnesses, and how extraordinary that total recall of four erased years cannot be silenced. How many places on the map were the meeting places, and what ruthless, cunning ingenuity brought those meetings about, the sight and smell and taste as the two strangers' bodies recognized one another beneath muffle of travel clothing in the arrival space of airports caged by the cicada shrill of foreign babble. How many hotel beds fallen to before even any suitcase or briefcase was opened. The bedside telephone where false names were answered to; an independent woman taking on in an hotel register that identity of a non-existent Mrs-So-and-So. The selective avoidance of restaurants where someone might show recognition, in London or Sydney or the remote hideout on some island. The address of a complicit friend of the man, a law firm to which a c/o letter from home would be sent when—in fact—the recipient received it forwarded to another city, another country. All this so vivid, along with the leisurely shared baths, he liked to exchange the intimacy of each soaping and exploring

the other's body, to end as a thrashing fucking. A night—
Warsaw, he had the brief of a dispute between Poles and
English clients—and there'd been a wonderful, stolen day
sight-seeing away in Cracow, she heard him use love-names
in a call to his wife, and beat her fists in jealousy against pillows, a reversion to angry childhood. How could it have been.
A successful lawyer in her forties, even if, as the man told
her, using another set of love-names, she had the breasts of a
twenty-year-old and the thought of her when he heard her
voice on the phone gave him an erection you wouldn't believe, such a hard-on. Don't avoid the way he would regale in
being caressed to ready him for a second entry after the first,
by the skilful hand on whose finger there was her wedding
ring. And was there a night—what pitiless, relentless totality
of all this come back—when he was in the hotel bar with a
friend of his family who mustn't know she was concealed in
the suite upstairs, and lying alone suddenly she was in cold
fear, was sure that something was wrong with Adrian, vision
of him dimmed by illness, disaster, and she sat up and dialled
home. It was not an hour he would be likely to be there. He
answered.

—Adrian.— The fearful loss of control in her voice must
have brought a certainty: this was a time when she was with
the man. Some months had passed since there had been one
of her professionally-required absences (Lyndsay has a case
in Namibia, your mother's in Toronto for a week).

He said out of that strange silence of distances, where
messages come from the grave: —Don't call me like this.—

She wept (blubbered like a stupid girl and could feel him
hearing the shamefulness of it). When she could speak:
—Don't be like this.—

Then she asked him about the son and daughters, whether the prearranged grocery orders from the suppliers were arriving regularly, and he gave the facts and said goodbye just as she was beginning, somehow, a plea of explanation—of what? Herself? What explanation was there? She had remarked—stated?—supposed to be a credo?—at the start of what seemed then only a double life to be managed, I am not a barnyard hen. She could count on his remembering the reference to a line from a favourite poet they had shared enthusiasm for when first they met. There must be a foothold left somewhere on the common ground of falling in love.

The man got rid of his old family friend and came back to embrace her in a hotel room that contained no echoes, neither of what it had just overheard nor of any other impassioned, angry, loving accusatory, conciliatory, triumphant, fruitless calls in its promiscuous service to couplings of occupants with fictitious names. He was not the kind to notice traces of emotions not roused by him.

The neurons and synapses are merciless in their uncontrollable selectivity. A secretary has to remind of names of clients whose cases were the subject of consultation only a year ago, perhaps. But nothing, nothing is inaccessible, avoidable, escapable in this case closed fifteen years ago. I have something to tell you.

It is all being told, all, no detail to be turned away from, presented by that self to the present self. Once upon a time. You found you were pregnant. To be factual the timing was such, a brief absence at a seminar and return home, that the error of conception could have been with husband or lover.

No female panic, neither man told of (once again) the blind opportunism of progeniture. Although abortion was illegal in those Calvinist regime days in her country, sister women always knew of out-of-the-way but competent if expensive doctors who would perform the simple procedure, and it was timely done. There was a complete family, daughters, a unique son; there was none of the sense of emptiness, regret for lost chance to bear a life that is supposed to depress a woman when she has that blob removed, to be done without as Paul has to do without a part of himself, one of the monitors of life. But now comes the fact that there is another fact of that time. Was it the chummy black nurse or the by now faceless doctor who told the blobs were two. Two foetuses waiting to grow into their human likenesses and be born. Well, twins come from the female line, her mother was a twin. Within a few days the man had entered her and Adrian had entered her. If not biologically possible—don't, don't give it scientific verity, don't join the lesser phenomena ranks of the late Dolly the Sheep—it is still a psychic reality in the emotion co-existent between contingent love and the love it is contingent to. In that unimaginable state of existence, the double conception is a reality.

This is a fantasy spewed of disgust. Self-disgust, a rising bile which apparently didn't affect that woman who was no barnyard hen. Flying free around the world. A man responded to at a duty dinner party just as her own young daughter, at the appropriate age, to the Brazilian as one of the mother's professional social obligations brought home. That woman, whoever she was, disembodied from the historical continuity of her life. Why did she not feel disgust, shame, then? Why

now, when there have been fifteen years to——that is the fashionable plaster for confession of political crimes——cleanse
and heal.

I have something to tell you.

Oh not all, though that is supposed to be the condition of
absolution.

I thought you were going to tell me you were leaving.

Truth and reconciliation. The one who offends, against
the power, as only the victim has, to open return to the historical continuity of a life.

Fifteen years have achieved this. There should be no need
to recognise the artifact of that four-year state of existence.
But it was an amputation, excision; admit it, four years cut
out of the time when he, Adrian, beloved, was in mid-life. The
loss is calculable now, only now, when he's about to enter that
half-life without the purpose of work. Even if its achievement was not his vocation. Four years taken from his maleness, the total capacity of love with all his being, the way
lovemaking was with him, not just fucking with penis and
tongue; love, with the cross-currents of children made by
that commitment, the being of a compound existence within
and against hazards of the world. Four years thrown in the
trash where contaminated paper plates go. And now this man
with his prostate humiliations and dimming deafness, soon
to withdraw with the books illustrating the vocation he gave
up (who knows if he would have fulfilled it) to the quarantine room transformed to that other confinement, 'retirement'——he cannot be given back those four years.

He talks of plans for a new phase of life to be entered
together.

To make up; make up to him for a state of self you cannot

understand could have existed—that's a childish notion. You cannot absolve yourself of the inconceivable. Nothing but to take up the acceptance into the historical continuity of life granted fifteen years ago. Cannot make up—to yourself— those four years you've deprived *yourself* of. What happened in that retrogression from all that was indispensable to you? The worst of ageing—fifty-nine if looking forty-nine—is you cannot know, find out. Why? How? Could you ever have interrupted your selfhood—yes—for an unthinking primitive gratification of some sort, a child gobbling a lollipop.

Who goes there . . .

The buzz from the intercom at the gate doesn't need any response asking identification of one seeking entry . . . it's Thapelo, he keeps a finger on the monitor as his fanfare greeting. They pull up their chairs in the garden, so many activities visualised in small boys' fantasy are succeeded by the visualised consequences of present reality. A bamboo-legged table has been commandeered to hold the spread of papers. Thapelo is spending some weeks on verification of actions being planned or taken behind closed doors by the Department of Minerals and Energy and the Department of Environmental Affairs, all their interconnections with industry, bidding consortia. Undercover stuff. Background to reports on the field research he and Derek were engaged in with Paul before—whatever this is, happened to him. And while Paul's inside (the word for jail seems the right one) there have been other environmental issues come up. —Yona ke yona! No limit to the way the construction companies khan'da!—

These words in the slang of his mother tongues (he speaks at least four or five) aren't italicised in Thapelo's talk, they belong in English just as his natural use of the scientific terms and jargon of his profession does. Or maybe they're part of the identification with his boyhood street life of blacks he asserts as essential to who and what he is. It's not what he's emancipated from: it's what he hasn't, won't leave behind.

So the scientist talks like a tsotsi when he pleases. That's how Paul teases him; in appreciation. Paul sums up in colloquialism common to black and white alike: no bullshit in Thapelo.

He comes both to keep his colleague informed and to consult with him; doesn't matter whether he's actually been delegated to do this by their employer organisation or it's something delegated by himself. The question of his continued exposure to Paul's Chernobyl—the nature of relations with officialdom in the work they do makes him dismissive of the controlling edicts of authority as hidden agenda. Paul's condition doesn't come up between them in their talk, interruptions of one another, laughter, lowered voices, shouts of emphasis, this garden resounds, echoes with the animation of its past. It's the quarters, now, where two men are absorbed in the work that informs their understanding of the world and their place as agents within it, from the perspective that everyone, like it or not, admit it or not, acts upon the world in some way. Spray a weed-killer on this lawn and the Hoopoe delicately thrusting the tailor's needle of its beak, after insects in the grass, imbibes poison. That's the philosophy of conservation from which Paul is approaching the great issues in a draft petition of an environmentalist coalition to the State President he's writing between discussions in the garden.

The pebble-bed nuclear experiment may be the apocalyptic one, *nuclear experiment you can walk away from*; there are also planned or proceeding slower means of development taking the form of destruction.

—So now it's the Australians in on the act. Haai! Pondoland, it's recognised all over the world, the centre of endemism, the great botanical treasure, n'swebu, man! The government wants to put a national toll highway through it, tear it up, and now they're going to let an Aussie company in to mine the dunes, destroy the coastline too. This Transworld Company says it's identified reserves there, sixteen million tons of heavy minerals and eight million tons of ilmenite. One of the biggest mineral sand deposits in the world. *Yesus!* This what we mean by attracting foreign investment? Mining on the beaches, same time the Minister of Tourism says the Germans, the Japanese and what-what flying in are big in our economic future—

Primrose has appeared with a tray of paper cups and the fruit juice prescribed for the one she cares for at some sort of distance decreed for her by her employers. She doesn't know where to put the burden and Thapelo interrupts himself, sweeps up the papers from the table, laughing and chaffing with her in what he's recognised, in an earlier encounter with her here in the garden, is her language among his four or five.

—The aspect for us to hammer—

Thapelo waves his cup across his colleague's half-sentence.
—The road and the mining are linked—like that, nê?— He bangs the flimsy cup, overflowing, down upon the table, clasps one fist in the other.

Invigorated by the piece of theatre, his colleague tries

again. —The aspect for us to go for is the broadest effect of danger the toll highway carries, pleas for beauty destroyed in these issues are regarded as going soft, just sentimental objection to progress—

—Chief, lalela, hear me, I think you're wrong there. You know that after mining tourism's our best income source. Who's coming to look at a mine, and a highway like they've got all over where they come from.—

—I'm talking about the Amadiba, my brother, they're living on the Wild Coast, five communities, not so? Go for *them*. From the plan you've shown me, the route of the highway plunges right through people's houses and fields, straight over their mealies. Staple food. What about the Amadiba Tribal Trust? Need to make them shout. Loudly. All stops out. Rally the traditional leaders; the government has to hear them; you know it's policy, government's having to recognise right now all kinds of questions on land distribution rights.—

—Derek's due down there next week.—

—And the National Road Agency? Any new statement from them? The figures they give for employment their grand highway will create—short-term, do they admit that.—

—The government must vuka! Open their eyes. See what's getting by in the name of development. All over the country. What about the cost of demissioning the pebble-bed plant? If it does light up that huge grid claimed, it can only last about forty years . . .—

The Hadedas landing from the house roof squawked derision. Their familiar companion took up quietly: —And the disposal of the nuclear waste. Where?—

Thapelo had brought photographs and surveyors' charts he had forgotten last time he came by. They bent over them, now and then, Thapelo constantly trespassing the distance at which his mate held him off, his forefinger returning to the toll highway, stabbing at a feature, the array spread among makeshift refreshment, coffee half-downed, the way they took it in the forest, in the bush, the desert. Thapelo had in a pocket—where was it, now—a pencil-length of root, shrunken and withered dead digit of a mangrove tree from the wetland they'd not long ago researched together, and the half-shell, patterned blue on cream like a fragment of Chinese porcelain, of a bird that would soon be extinct. Thapelo had the habit of absently gathering such small signs as he walked. When he was there, the garden was an enclave, paused at together, a wilderness.

Thapelo had left.

The eggshell and root, there on the table.

How many more days go by in the garden.

There are markers other than time on the way back from this state of existence. Not all are reassuring. Not without confusion. Yes, the doctors had given the cancer all clear. Only: after some months—How many months?—A shrug; somewhere between three and six, we'll do a scan. That's all. A precautionary follow-up. Most unlikely, but it can be that another radioactive treatment is indicated in some cases.

But now, so far as radioactivity is concerned? He is no longer radiant. All clear.

He hears otherwise, from his body.

His decision is to remain a week or so in a kind of halfway—between the leper refuge and the return, harmless to the human fold. How could Benni question this protection

of her and the child; how could Adrian and Lyndsay be seen
to think his presence become a burden? And he was still
weak. Wobbly due to lack of muscle tone, the inactivity of
weariness, the spell cast in the pursuit of rabid cells on the
loose in his body. He had to get to know that body again; the
doctors were aware of this consequence, of course, and it was
arranged that a masseur would come to revive his depleted
flesh before he quit the old family home once again in his
life-cycle. A man arrived, about his own age, the thirties, neither young nor near the barrier of the forties. The man chat-
tered amiably as he worked, first with the body laid out on its
back, his strong hands cool at contact, warm as he went over
the chest, triceps, biceps, diaphragm area, moved down to the
thighs and calves. Body belly-down. Massage of the feet, that
was the beginning; the significance of biblical washings of
the feet, a sacred tending to the most distant part of physical
awareness, least emotive. Unless the shoes pinch or a thorn
pricks, barefoot, who notices what's carrying you. Sometimes
in bed the foot of one nuzzles for a moment the foot of the
other but that happenstance has little to do with caresses of
the body. 'He kisses their feet'—a derogatory reference to
sycophancy. The deft and firm manipulation of the feet brings
to notice, like the existence of someone who had gone ignored, the expressive mobilities in the curve of arch and key-
board of toes; so this is what took over, came into play—what
one danced. What was prehensile when a boy climbed the
jacaranda. Up calves and thighs, the hands brought back the
good tensions of effort, sensation of running through thick
underbrush, taut balancing over stones. Then the hard-smooth
palms and fingers came up the outer sides of the buttocks,
down and up over to the spine, and along either side of that

stem and back again, down. The man was leaning over, when his hands reached the muscular contour of the upper back and shoulders—that male attribute, secondary only to the frontal display between the legs—his breath just touched on the bare nape of the neck. Massage is hard work, deep breaths are audible, their touch is a soft breeze.

How long since he had come alive like this with Berenice/Benni. The growing, brimming against the resistance of the hard surface on which he lay face down. What had deserted him with the emanations of that unseen light, the ordinary birthright phenomenon he had wondered if he would ever again wake with in the morning. His erect penis, that other self of a man, restored to him.

Under the hands of a man.

Never had a sexual relation with a *doppelgänger*, a replica of myself: that's how he sees the act. No homophobia, either, each to his or her own sexual instincts; he's attracted to women and although there's enough evidence they're attracted to him—advances to be read even from among his wife's friends—men evidently were not. No gay proposals although his working life is intimately and virtually exclusively among his own sex.

So unquestioning about himself.

This question coming now.

Take what he is feeling as the last alienation of that state of existence.

It was decided he would *leave home* this second time to go *home* as an adult, at a weekend, when everyone would be free to welcome and settle him in, there.

Decided by his mother and his wife, each representative of those habitats. He was not yet reaccustomed to taking practical decisions for himself. If his radiance had gone dark he was not ready, after so long under orders of others, for sunlight, except that of the garden. During his last days he kept what since the visits of Thapelo had been something like a routine, worked in that place of outdoor activity most of the day on the material Thapelo brought him.

Going home: home that is work to be done. The pebble-bed nuclear reactor project is neither abandoned nor finally approved, in the holding silence like that which falls over international inquiry into the possession of nuclear capabilities in certain countries. The thought is troubling: research must be continued to be used for protest as vigorously as possible to keep the issue alive.

There was the possibility he might be ready to go with his team on another field research at present in its planning stage. When the wilderness received him he would believe the oncologists' guarded edict that he was all clear, belonged among humankind, animals, birds, reptiles, insects, trees and plants without taint or threat. The project was one for which Thapelo piled more and more documentation, including tape recordings of contesting opinions on feasibility from chemical engineers, social scientists, anyone and everyone concerned with environmental management, the professionals along with the Greens, Save The Earth, Earthlife, International Rivers Network—campaigners of all titles and acronyms.

A dam. Ten dams.

A conventional developmental concept this time. Old as when the earliest agriculturists rolled stones into a stream to block its flow for themselves. Not the pebble-bed experiment descended from deadly alchemy of atoms that can achieve space-fiction in reality. But as the nuclear plant is promised to light vast areas of powerless darkness, the great dams are promised to gather water to slake the thirst of human populations and the industries which employ and feed them.

The Okavango is an inland delta in Botswana, the country of desert and swamp landlocked in the middle of the breadth of South West, South and South East Africa. That's it on the maps; nature doesn't acknowledge frontiers. Neither can ecology. The consequences of what happens to the inland delta affect the region. How far?

The surveyors' sheets, both actual and speculative, represent the phenomena; as they are now.

Maze of waterways remembered as the glide of a narrow boat through passages between skyscraper reeds made by hippopotami, their local streets and lanes. Berenice was in the boat; not what she dubs with some due acknowledgement in her throwaway laughter, a macho bushboys' assignment. He thought he was fairly familiar with the ecosystem, at the time, had read up a bit to refresh this colloquially so she could share something of the wilderness he was fortunate to experience completely; while she had only her terrain of a city. But no—no reminiscent holiday snapshot album—a compilation of dossiers overlapping, having to be held down against the riffling of garden breeze by a stone on the bamboo-legged table: he realised he knew too abstractly, himself limited by professionalism itself, too little of the grandeur and delicacy, cosmic and infinitesimal complexity of an ecosystem complete as this. The Okavango could never have been planned on a drawing-board by the human brain. Its transformations, spontaneous, self-generated, could not have been conceived. And this is no evidence to be claimed by religious or other creational mysticism, either. The innovation of matter is greater than that of any collective of minds, faiths. As Thapelo would say, Yona ke yona—this is it! The capacity to visualise this complex, let alone create it, as *a project* of a multinational team of genius hydrologist engineers is as limited in scale as taking the hippo's part in maintaining the system as something that can be understood without the to-and-fro, in-and-out, problem-solving of the infinite whole. The Okavango delta in co-existence with a desert is a system of elements contained, maintained—by the phenomenon itself, unbelievably, inconceivably. The Okavango is a primal feature of creation, so vast it can be seen by astronauts from Outer Space. This is an excitement that must be confirmed—he has to leave the garden of isolation to go into the house and dial Thapelo.

Where to begin understanding what we've only got a computerspeak label for, *ecosystem*? Where to decide it begins. Let's say, the known point at which we grasp its formation is where the rivers and streams converge and the patterns of their flow—meeting, opposing—create islands out of the sand they carry, landscapes within the waterscape. Trees grow; where do the seeds come from to germinate them, does the water bring detritus roots which find new foothold? If we identify the tree species, you'll learn from how far and from where water journeys have brought them? What journeys! They have brought sand and it's leached from along its routes, salt. Six hundred and sixty tons a year! That's the figure! In that calm delta disturbed only by the hippos and crocodiles, evaporation in an area bordering on a desert is extreme.

The salt content becomes high; contamination problem, ay. Yebo! But no. Managed by matter itself. Trees suck up the water to the islands for growth. Salt comes with it. The sand filters the brackish stuff: clean water flows back, supports fish and the predators of fish, the crocs, hippos, fish eagles.

—Cho! Ayeye! You're forgetting something, Chief. Didn't you read? Eventually the salt kills the trees, there's nothing to hold the island, it disintegrates, back into the water—

—Yes, but there's some formation of peat, and with the next rainy season the rivers come down again—

—From Angola from—

—The sand blocks channels in the reeds and papyrus, there're islands forming again, saplings sprouting again, it's been happening who knows how long?—

—Tuka! The salt? So what happened to the salt.—

—Exactly, we don't know how the salt is managed. *It is.* Probably seeps down through underground watercourses with increasing dilution and is widely dispersed in acceptable levels way through other areas of the region, part of the whole Southern Continental system. We drink that water! This's what we should work on, how with the Okavango the balance between positive and negative is achieved . . .—

—You think that'll change their minds about building the dams. Eish!—

—My brother—the dams are total negations. All this beautifully managed balance will be wrecked. Forever. There should be a category. Destructive Development, closed corporation of disaster. We're chronically short of water and it's not understood that this—what, phenomenon, marvel, much, much more than that—this intelligence of matter, receives, contains, processes, finally distributes the stuff God knows how far, linking up with other systems. If you and I decide now, how it begins, how it works, it still has no end, no dam walls, it's living. And some fucking consortium's going to drain, block and kill what's been *given*, no contracts.—

The blurt of laughter is the colleague's welcome at hearing a man at least sounding restored from the stricken substitute for himself found in the garden.

—Phambili! Top form! We're not going to let them get away with it. Woza!—

Forever.

The receiver replaced, the laughter silenced. Adrenalin that (like that other bodily signal) hadn't risen for so long, sinks normally. Still addressing—Thapelo or self—something slowly enters as a third voice, insistent to be heard. Follows, to the garden. And then back to the telephone; is the machine staring mute, or being gazed at, unseeing. But it's not picked up. There are areas of thought not meant to be shared, they question certainties held in common. Neither of you could go on pursuing what you do, being what you are, without them.

Forever.

How long is forever. How old is the delta that is part of the cosmos visible from Outer Space? Astronauts report it. Will ten dams be visible, the scale of ponds, like all manmade scratchings and gougings in comparison with the planet's own design.

Maybe we see the disaster and don't, can't live long enough (that is, through centuries) to see the survival solution Matter with infinite innovation has found, finds, will find, to renew its principle—life: in new forms, what we think is gone *forever*. In millennia, what does it count that the white rhino becomes extinct, the dinosaur's extinct, the mastodon, the mammoth, but we have the ingenuity of the evolved design of the giraffe, the elephant with its massive hulk standing vestigially web-footed with the memory of the fish. The first fish that dragged itself out of the amniotic element.

So, what is this kind of stuff, thinking . . . Heresy, how can it come to one who when asked, And what is your line, answers, What am I, I'm a conservationist, I'm one of the new missionaries here not to save souls but to save the earth.

This heresy is born of the garden, as Evil was—like those other thoughts, to be forgotten, the garden engendered—it belongs to this state of existence that's about to cease to be. Whatever 'forever' means, irrevocably lost, or surviving eternally, himself in this garden is part of the complexity, the necessity. As a spider's web is the most fragile example of organisation, and the delta is the grandest. Return home; that's his loop in the thread from the spider's web to the Okavango system: Benni/Berenice, small boy, Daddy! Paul! all the waterways and shifting sand islands of contradiction: a condition of living. Like another heresy, knowledge of what it is he came from into this state of existence, and what—if he survived—he would be returned to—the relationships of that home were not what he might have had; knows that. Doubt had come to him in the garden where he had begun to apprehend life as a boy. Biodiversity; *Chief,* say to yourself: professional jargon stuff. But it's within that term your place is, *Chief,* say it: I'm going home at the weekend. Always find the self calling on the terminology of the wilderness, so unjudgmental, to bring to circumstances the balm of calm acceptance. The inevitable grace, zest, in being a microcosm of the macrocosm's marvel.

Doubt is part of it; the salt content.

They are there at the gate. Berenice——but he must correct himself, Benni again——and the small boy, Nicholas, his son.

Lyndsay and Adrian are his entourage as he emerges from the family house, with Primrose helping to carry some of the things——folders of papers accumulated recently——that wouldn't fit into the suitcase Adrian insists on carrying. (The hospital hold-all Lyndsay has quietly disposed of.) They call out to one another across the length of the drive as if it were the length of time of the separation. Even Primrose, with her old-fashioned servitude, pre-liberation sense of propriety that you could be familiar with white kids as you should not with adults, shouted to the child joyfully ——So now soon you'll come to play with me, like always, Nickie!—— But there can be nothing ordinary about this approach to the gate. It's Benni who's clinging, arms lifted, to the bars this time. Smiling and cajoling——as if he needed any encouragement! He doesn't disappoint her, finds himself gathering the muscles, co-ordination.

She——Benni——sees coming towards her the long legs flung out sideways at the knees, the arms flailing like oars, the staggering gait, that of a child learning it can run.

As he gained the gate the electronic control in Adrian's hand slid it open, Benni's image brought close-up to him with the pressure of her arms around his body: she was laughing, the lens of tears magnifying her eyes. She reached for his head and took his lips, mouth, into hers as a deep draft of something missing so long. But when he knelt to the small boy, his son stared at him a moment and turned away to hide behind his mother. Not forgotten, fingers prized from the bars of this gate, *Daddy! Paul!,* and the appeal terribly unheeded. Agitated, ashamed, his mother tried to urge him forward, he wriggled and struggled, ran back behind her.

It was understood: his son had suffered that state of existence, along with himself.

—No, leave him, it's all right. Give him time.—

iii / *It Happens*

Success sometimes may be defined as a disaster put on hold. Qualified. Has to be. The pebble-bed reactor project has not been abandoned by the entrepreneurs but it hasn't gone further than being claimed safe enough to walk away from. In the meantime there had been the other experience of the phenomenon of these small natural formations during a return to the normal custom of a couple taking their child to enjoy a week paddling and dabbling on a beach. *Daddy! Paul!* showing him how to collect the colours of land and sea in the shining pebbles sucked over by rills of surf.

The direst of all threats in the world's collective fear— beyond terrorism, suicide bombings, introduction of deadly viruses, fatal chemical substances in innocent packaging, Mad Cow disease—is still 'nuclear capability'. Another catch-all: the possession as natural resources, in a country, of certain primary elements and the ability to mine and refine these for its own nuclear armament or for sale to that of others; the construction of a nuclear plant/reactor; the testing of a

...ear weapon. Forecast prelude to the apocalypse by what ...re known as Weapons of Mass Destruction. The proposed reactor based on the harmless pebble a small boy takes home from the beach is a component in the production of Weapons not likely to be overlooked by the inquiry into nuclear facilities that is becoming vigilant all over the world, far if not near, since the power with a foot on everyone's doorstep, the USA, is one that doesn't support the nuclear non-proliferation requirement of efforts towards nuclear disarmament, except when this suits USA ambitions. Thapelo drops in over a weekend on the pretext, just to check up on you (they're back working together at their organisation's offices during the week) but really to analyse Gaddafi's sudden decision to announce and renounce Libya's possession of nuclear capability.

Tell all. Come clean, brother. Haai, ma-an!

Neither sees any mystery in the decision. They laugh at the 'amazement' on newspaper headlines. Gaddafi either doesn't want American guests like the ones who've visited Iraq or he wants the embargo, imposed after his countrymen exploded a passenger plane, lifted so he can sell his oil. Or both.

But under the laughter the mates now may have some expectation an example has been set—and received with fulsome emotion from the world—that might lead to the pebble-bed reactor project being taken off hold and abandoned, for State reasons of adopting moral high ground, or rather choosing to stay up there since South Africa is a signatory to the nuclear non-proliferation treaty. There's somehow always been little socialising with Paul's colleagues, by contrast with hers, so Berenice/Benni sees the animating Sunday visit of this colleague as part of Paul's new return to his life and takes the opportunity of inviting his apparently special friend to share lunch.

Lively dialogue continues. Other projects on hold while being developed discreetly are the national toll highway through the Wild Coast, that great botanical treasure of endemism, crop lands of subsistence farmers; the mining concession for the sand dunes and——the dams. The ten dams. The Okavango. As astronauts grasp from Outer Space the beauty of this cosmic scale of waterways, so its existence as an ecological world phenomenon has become clear to international environmental agencies from their perspective down on earth. Paul since his return to work has been delegated by his team to research and prepare a study of the region. He's the one to meet the representatives from Save The Earth and the International Rivers Network who come to see for themselves what can be understood from the perspective with your feet on the ground, as a site of planned destruction important to world ecology.

He has been back. Back home: a wilderness. Accompanying these people who represent international concern. He was utterly renewed in watching, listening, storing their responses to the glory of the complex not even the mysteries of the imagination, the subconscious, could conjure, so that the assurance he had had in his radiant isolation that he would be restored to himself with a return to the wilderness, was subsumed if not needed to be remembered.

One of those women, often scientists, who look as if they have never been children and are in an indeterminate age for a lifetime, spoke aside to him rather than her colleagues. ——How marginal, demeaned, remote . . . I don't know . . . left out of it.— And another in the group, a man, murmured in the slowly extinguishing light of early evening, You feel . . .—

Hearing this apparently general reaction to overwhelment by splendour beyond skylines he doesn't tell, no, you have to endure being in it: a menacing part of it. Its evil genius: enterprise from Australia, private and state hubris in Africa.

How are things going? A friend at the Agency risks as an afterthought to presenting copy for a cosmetics brand campaign. Does she mean, is the husband quite well again. Or does she unknowingly ask the question, is he himself again. Berenice takes the hesitant, kindly-meant enquiry in the second, unspoken sense.

Benni is particularly affectionate and carefully considerate with Paul, as one is, would be, with anyone who had been seriously ill. Rather, has come back from a life-threatening experience of some kind, any kind. Hijack, plane crash, earthquake. This of his was no ordinary illness; she comes to know more and more, day by day, night by night, in self-perceptions of unease. Making love is surely the ultimate in the enactment of loving, in the eagerly generous response he must find in entering her body he will find himself again. As he used to be. They make love more often than ever. She is ashamed, even to admit deeply buried within her awareness, she has some fear that what enters her, what is enveloped by her dark clasping passageway, carries some alien light, still. Denial of the fear makes her the one who initiates caresses if he has not, putting her hand on his penis when he is already

half into sleep. With time the shaming fear disappears under
intense pleasure and its expectation of being experienced again
and again. This man who has come back to her, whoever he
is, makes love . . . how to explain it to herself, best leave it
alone—as if each is the last in his life. So he must be happy?
Her work sensibly defines satisfaction of one kind or another
as happiness, persuading people that to buy a new-model car
or luxury cruise tickets is to satisfy a need to be happy. He has
never been particularly communicative, gregarious as she is,
drawing attention and company; the attraction of opposites—
well-known—evident in their marriage. Yet she feels that
what happened to him maybe means he must instinctively
move towards contact with others, now, not confined with his
acolyte bushmates in the emptiness of the wilderness; come
to life in the variety of friends and stimulating jostle of lively
acquaintances she and many other intelligent—yes—people
enjoy. To bring this about as what appears naturally, she includes that rather charming bushmate of his, Thapelo—
cool!—who wasn't even afraid to go and sit with him in his
untouchable quarantine—in drinks parties and occasional
dinners with a mix of colleagues and even clients, some of
whom are really interesting people in fields of know-how
that surely would intrigue anyone. Paul's real closeness, outside the bed, is of course with their small boy, he reads to
Nickie during the times when in his absence she used to set
the kid up before children's TV programmes, makes things
with him out of bits of fruit boxes, joins in the games when
Nickie's friends come round to play. The young mothers
looking on tell her she's lucky, the man's a great father.
Between field trips he goes alone for his blood tests at the

laboratory. She chooses the right moment to ask if every-thing was all right. He tells her the doctors say so.

And you? And you?

But then it comes to her unbidden, as the fear did, she has the strange knowing that he, personally, is not responsible to her. Has decided this.

So that's how things are going.

There is Christmas without the parents. They have gone away on the postponed holiday. That means there is no pres-ence in reminder of the quarantine; it is Christmas with the lit-up tree and greedy excitement of the child, a festival like everyone else's, and there's the New Year, baptised with cham-pagne from a liquor chain whose advertising account Berenice handles, a year that the man of the family has lived to see.

Adrian and Lyndsay have not gone on the trip to the frozen northlands he had thought of as an example of the new ventures of retirement. They are in Mexico. That is also a venture never before taken. Lyndsay was delighted with his switch of continents and climates. I'm not thick-skinned enough for below zero! Mexico in late autumn to winter, along their itinerary, was like winter at home on the highveld, cold at night and ideally warm at midday. It's not an organised tour rounded up by sheepdog guides, but as neither speaks nor understands Spanish they found within the first day that to enjoy fully what you're seeing after getting yourself to sites, it would be good to have a local English-speaking per-son with you instead of keeping your nose stuck in the dingy prose of a guide book. The porter at their Mexico City hotel had a discussion, private since it was in Spanish, with the doorman, called up something on his computer and presented a name and a telephone number. This one is for you. Very excellent. He searched for a personality sufficiently famous to testify to this, and invented if not recalled, Wife of American President was one time going round with her. The recommended guide turned out unexpectedly but happily to be a Scandinavian whose clear English with its definitively enunciated final *t* and *d*, over the phone, was matched by an equally clear knowledge of the history—archaeological, architectural, cultural, political—of where they stood on each site and what they were seeing there; what was before them in palaces, museums, colossal fragments and exquisitely delicate jewellery, all of the ancient past.

She drove them in her Volvo to Cuernavaca and in Guadalajara to stand beneath the Rivera murals (on postcards to each of their daughters and their son Lyndsay wrote how, when she was a student articled to a law firm, she had bought with her first earnings as a weekend waitress a cheap print of Rivera's girl with arum lilies). They climbed the great pyramids without getting too out of breath, explained to the admiring Norwegian that this was because they came from a high-altitude city at home, were accustomed to rarefied air. The guide was admiring of everything, of the phenomenon of life itself, smiling ruthlessly, a kind of well-being, even to be seen in profile by whoever (taking turns) sat beside her while she drove. She was well-rounded but not the obligatory Scandinavian blue-eyed blonde, careless curly dark hair blew back or played tendrils on her pink forehead. Smiling was the natural muscular conformation of her face evidently, even when she was not talking or listening in response. A person with a happy nature, born like that, Lyndsay remarked as she and Adrian summed up the experience of the second day with their unexpected find. Who knows, Adrian said. And of course, the professional archaic smile is part of the tourist guide's package. Anyway she was a pleasant accompaniment, extremely useful to their venture. She was even worldly, intelligent enough to want to be told something of their own country, how it had changed since the end of apartheid (she pronounced the word correctly)—but then Norwegians, people from comfortably stable regions always have an interest, concern born of their contrasting good luck, perhaps, for countries great in area and conflict. Both of them must have had the passing thought, during these happy days of venture, how did this Scandinavian come to be a guide in Mexico. Just because she was fluent in Spanish and English? But there was no wish to be distracted, by a stranger's personal history, from the fascination of the specialised knowledge of medicine in a lost civilisation evidenced by instruments in a glass showcase, and the huge unfurlment of the Ambras Emerald—feather head-dress tall as any man who might have been exalted enough to wear it. These spectacles were on the site, in the place they continued to prize best and return to of all others, famous, or some obscure but known to one as serenely experienced as their Norwegian. This place was the Museum of Anthropology back in Mexico City, inadequately named they at once discovered, for the Dantesque journey through not only the evolution of the human being but on to an unsurpassed achievement of certain skills.

—And hubris.— Adrian's remark as Lyndsay took his hand in confirmation of what they were experiencing together.

Then they were walking the length of the Teotihuacán plumed serpent uncoiled, grey-green. They had seen so many colours and textures hewn from the millennial formations of mountains, and transformed into another, human version of the Creation. Jadeite? Adrian guessed, and was gently corrected by their guide. —Polychrome. It's a full-scale model of the original, too huge to transport, sixth to eighth century A.D.— They were distracted by a giant Mayan eagle above them, unmistakably stone, with menacing beak open in full cry. When they were resting on their hotel bed before dinner Lyndsay was to say that the statement of colossi, relics of an exalted civilisation that Cortés and his successors toppled, came to her suddenly with Adrian's *And hubris* as a flashback of the plane plunging into the second of the World Trade Center towers.

Adrian dozing: Of course, we understand the present a bit better by knowing the past.

Of course: Adrian, missed vocation in archaeology.

What they had both lingered before, irresistible and oddly stirring, was a cinema-sized screen of juxtaposed images, like a series of enlarged passport photographs. But the images were not static, fixed. Each was a skull that changed in the next take and the next, the blink of the camera of time, the bone structure modified, angles and emphasis receded, re-aligned, flesh-covering emerged, shaping nose, outlining the apertures of eyes and mouth, then flick-flick—a generic human face evolving into a recognisable one: Asiatic, Caucasian, Negroid, the round eyes, the epicanthal folds, the arched nose, the malleable-looking broad flat one, the soft everted lips, the straight thin line in which others meet.

Passport photographs of more than one's ancestry back to

a common design of bone. Lyndsay was unaccustomedly loud-voiced although there were other tourists around: —It's a kind of DNA!— And they stood unable to leave the exhibit, now quietly, amusedly pointing out to each other, youngsters exchanging secrets, look how that one's exactly like so-and-so, that one definitely tells that so-and-so has Japanese blood somewhere. And what about us, mmh? Each born of the Western European type that had been two or three generations in Africa; isn't there likely to be some mutation, detail of feature or flesh that records entry of a black strain, not just the evolutionary effect of climate and elements of nouriture. And the juxta-presence of other strains, Malays, Indians, Chinese, all come to Africa over generations. They must take a new good look at the face of the other in the nakedness of a shared bathroom, when he's exposed, freshly shaven, and make-up has been creamed-off her public image. The guide stands by smiling. She must've seen it all numerous times before; *she* is not quite recognisable, anyway, as the definitive Scandinavian type. Mixed exotic interruptions, not an unbroken lineage—what about the Vikings? Their ventures? Great voyagers, maybe their encounters mixed the blood-stock of ancestry. Lyndsay is so rousedly interested that Adrian says to her, not remembering that once she used to say to him, You would have made a good lawyer—You would have been a good anthropologist.— At least as an avocation, like archaeology, but of course law was both vocation and avocation, for her. And with the smiling onlooker, they laughed. Over lunch Adrian offered at a Chinese restaurant their guide recommended (unexpected find in Mexico, like herself), she said with her way of stretching her soft full throat and turning her head back and to one side, they were the most enthusiastic people she'd taken around for years. A compliment is always pleasing. They raised their glasses of Chinese beer to her expertise and tact.

Lyndsay had an important case coming up, one of those arising out of a government agency's inquiries into corruption between government officials, highly-placed politicians, and what is collectively called private enterprise, which includes cabinet members—stockholders in the businesses of their cousins and in-laws. She had to return to prepare with her partners the defence of one of the accused. Adrian knew better than to ask if she really believed the man was not guilty. But he thought it absolutely unnecessary for her to have to return while she was enjoying their new venture so much; why couldn't her partners do without her for once. What did she have partners for, if one could not stand in for another who had worked so hard and selflessly for years. He did not refer to the leave she had taken for frequent absences overseas, those years ago. So long ago.

This was not a conference, it was a case of important moral significance to the government of their country! *He* was in the preparatory phase of his retirement, didn't he realise he was free at last. Freed to follow, for once, his avocation, in a country where there were archaeological sites you wouldn't find among the Makapan Caves and the dig where Mrs later identified as Mr Ples lay for millennia. The Norwegian they'd found compatible enough could take him to archaeological sites while he stayed on for a couple of weeks.

But you?

I'm a big girl . . . You wouldn't be seeing much of me anyway, the case's going to be heard in Bloemfontein.

They made love the night before she left. She said as they

turned to sleep, under brief emotion difficult to control—heaven knows why, because the statement was in line with their plans for retirement—This probably will be my last big case, it'll drag on to the end, end of the year. As if as she spoke, a decision was made. The Mexican venture was only the first of those they were going to take, free together.

Benni knew from her Berenice experience in the public relations of advertising that black men in business generally left their wives at home when they came to cocktail parties and even dinners, the empty place beside them in the seating arrangements at official functions being cleared of cutlery, glasses, by a waiter, and in a private house dealt with by a shift-up closer of those seated. A black entrepreneur might bring a beautiful girlfriend along, on the side, made known only by her first name, barely introduced on the general understanding she wasn't really there.

There was Paul's return to the bush with his team of black as well as white mates—and you held your breath or didn't think about it: he seemed absolutely restored to strength enough to go out and live rough. The other factor was the relationship with their child. (Her friends remarking, what a good father, lucky you.) It was so normal, familial—after all that had happened—he had never confessed the deprivation, those times they sat apart, facing one another in the quarantine garden, the grown man's childhood, the past. Wouldn't it be part of what she ought to do to restore life in him, bring children and wives of his Thapelos, not just the ecological bushmates alone, home to the house, as a natural expression of what ordinary life is now that the colour you are doesn't

compose it. So not just restore him; there's the unexamined
sense that life can never be as it was. Something the new man
may need to bring a new kind of relationship into the old one
(left in the garden) that served—the attraction of opposites.
Saturday braai on the terrace seems the occasion to invite
Derek and Thapelo with emphasis that this includes wives
and children. The mix of a few friends from the Agency includes a black photographer with his Afro-American girlfriend and a lesbian copywriter (white) who is surprised by
the arrival of the dishy husband's bushmates, Thapelo and
Derek.

—I wouldn't have thought as they prefer living away
miles from anywhere their idea of pleasure would be to come
back to all these swarming kids.—

Her Agency mate Berenice laughed at her over the salad
they were making.

—You'll never understand what it means to be straight,
my innocent darling. Get a life!—

Derek has four children and Thapelo three on their legs
and a baby in a padded carry-cot decked with dangling toys.
Derek's wife manages to look like the sexually challenging
teenager she must have been, with nipples poking at a T-shirt
but the set of years is in the angle of the cigarette in her
mouth. Thapelo's is a beauty, a schoolteacher who could be
one of the models in Berenice's campaigns to promote luxury
cars or cosmetics. The tossing blond hair of Derek's woman,
placing her as a sister rather than mother to her twelve-
year-old daughter casting about her blond veil in the same
way, is completed in contemporary fashionableness by the
braided and beaded heads of Thapelo's woman and six-year-
old daughter. The bushmates, including Paul—Berenice has

no false modesty, existence is too ruthless for that—apparently go for showy species outside as well as inside the wilderness.

The children, for whom pizzas have been provided, race about in rivalry, covet one another's toys, invent games, hug lovingly, tussle savagely and have to be parted. The private schools they go to, these days, have black and white pupils and all the complexions and features characteristic of in-between colours; there is nothing unexpected for them in this gathering.

Who would have thought of the intellectually efferves-cent Thapelo—cool—as a family man. Here he is with the young climbing all over him. He shares, mouth by mouth turnabout, his piled plate with his younger daughter, steadies her on legs that have only recently begun to take her weight. Nicholas goes, as if in the superiority of his age making a claim to match, to hang on Paul's shoulder he can reach where his father is hunkered on the grass.

The three men who live another life in the wilderness cannot be together in any company without evoking it in references, discussion, argument between them, out of which every now and then they turn a passionate (rhetorical) question or a challenge of fact that ought to be known to the others around who surely don't know and maybe don't want to. But the company has been chosen expressly by Berenice-as-Benni to bring them—something—together, and her selection works well because the listening copywriter looks alternately sceptical, then attentively in agreement, and the photographer and the American break in or over the voices of the bushmates.

—What doesn't get published except in scientific-speak Mrs Jones or Mr Tshabalala don't understand, aren't meant to, is that those radioactive isotopes could fall into wrong hands, make black bombs radioactive—

The American has a voice insistent as a doorbell. —What the hell—oh *hell*, sure—is a 'black bomb'? I'm one of those dumb folk who don't hear you right.—

Her boyfriend must assert he's not with her there, he's a professional photographer in the advertising industry, he gets around, and he's a South African. —They're talking about Koeberg, the nuclear thing in the Cape.—

—No—these're some facts of the risks of a pebble-bed reactor that's high up on the planning board.—

—Well, you could say hugely adjunct to existing dangers of Koeberg, Derek.— Paul, animated on the familiar ground of grim reference, is addressing himself, with a droll distortion of his mouth, aside to the uninitiated.

—Look at these kids. Our kids. All our kids. D'you know about the danger, what babies could breathe in from the day they're born. Never mind all the security that's going to be installed.— Thapelo adds for the understanding of his mates alone—*You can walk away from it.* Shaya-shaya!—

The photographer throws up open palms. —All of us here are supposed to believe this.—

—So how far along is this pebble reactor thing, I mean is it in the works now?—

Doesn't the woman—Benni's told Paul the photographer's girlfriend is in banking—read the newspapers while she's visiting a country. Well we all follow only what we think affects us personally, soccer results or maybe with her it's the

New York Stock Exchange and interest rates; now, it's better not to go further than the date of the next blood tests. He tells her what's at least been published for everyone to learn. —Eskom, that's the government's Electricity Supply Commission, got a licence from the National Nuclear Regulator before the end of last year. Although the Environmental Affairs Minister was challenged in court by Earthlife Africa and other groups, even the Cape Chamber of Commerce—businessmen who've usually got other things on their calculators than extinction by nuclear leaks . . .—

—I can't believe it's as bad as that. As near.— The copywriter has stopped eating the vegetarian meal her colleague Berenice provided for her; but she can't take a clean breath, away from the smoke off the meat over fire.

Thapelo has been coaxed to his feet by the one who is just learning to use hers and is dancing African-style with her. —That's the problem, we can't get people to believe. That's why Eskom's big bosses have been allowed by the government to spend one billion on developing the pebble-bed technology.—

The photographer heaves up from his sprawl and presents himself to the three ordinary-looking fellow males who seem to speak as voices from the mouths of biblical prophets. —Look, I'd be interested in taking pictures of these sites, I mean, the place the thing's going to be.—

To lighten the mood Benni calls from where she's turning the chops. —I don't think the subject's saleable as a promotion to any of our clients, dear Lemeko!—

Perhaps nobody hears her above the sizzling.

—What else do you do out there? According to Berenice she doesn't see Paul for weeks.—

Derek refills his wineglass with an eyebrow-raise asking permission from anyone who happens to be looking, and says, as if it were a confession: —Well, here's something else. There's a strong coalition campaigning to stop a new national highway from being sliced through the Pondoland Coast, incredibly rich botanically. Ever been there? We work on background scientific research to make protest based on absolutely undeniable facts. Try for what's unchallengeable. That toll highway must never be; for the plant-life and the people-life—the Amadiba live there.—

The copywriter remembers reading something interesting recently about—what was it—a world heritage site called 'The Cradle of Mankind'—are the three doing anything concerned with that?

The host moves to do what he ought to be concentrating on, tending the trough of embers and taking over the turning of meat, but delays. —Thirteen dolomite limestone caves. Fossil remains of plants, animals, and hominids—they're early members of the human family. It's not our field. You can't do anything to save the dead. But you sh'd go and get a sense of these places, the nearest is quite close to us in Johannesburg. I'd like to take Benni and Nickie, you could come along.—

—I'm afraid of bats.— She was flirtatious on wine although she had no desire to attract men.

Australopithecus, distant relative: told of that in childhood by his father. *Paranthropus*, not ancestral to the living people gathered on this Saturday, but an evolutionary adaptation (remembered it like a litany) that lasted in Africa for a million years. And the Pleistocene period relating to the time between the ice age and the beginning of humans; Adrian's passion, amateur palaeontologist, anthropologist, archaeologist. So knowledgeable, and the son who listened to him became equally dedicated but in another 'field'. Professionally, life-work, not a retirement hobby.

The gathering stayed on until early dark. The sunset was spectacular because of pollution in the air, according to Derek—everyone laughed at him for spoiling the effect, better be ignorant of some phenomena. —Anyway, you can't sell anything any more by using the good old riding-off-into-the-sunset image. Get a life!— Benni spoke up happily derisively for her colleagues. This venture went well. Nickie became quite wild, little king who had found companions. When the friends left, she and Paul cleaned up together. She watched him for signs of fatigue she thought, not because any doctor had suggested it, would question his recovery, his return. But he looked fine; in bed she smelled in his hair the homely smoke of the feast he'd duly tended.

Was it Berenice or Benni who proposed it.

The two personae were more and more mingled in the life they lived now. It was certainly after the several months following that Saturday, months during which there were the same kind of easy invitations in response to her trial one; she was asked by her Agency colleagues to bring along those nice bushmates of Paul, Thapelo and Derek whatsisname, with their kids, and Thapelo and his wife Thandike in return included the copywriter (who was this time accompanied by her woman), the photographer and his American girlfriend, to celebrate a birthday in Thapelo's family.

Let's have a baby.

Another child. She did not tell him it was even a career decision; she was prepared to lose some of her energy, her drive towards success after success, to give her body over to the disadvantages of distortion and accept the distracting, absorbing emotions of loving care for an infant.

—It's right for Nickie. An only child—that's lonely.—

God knows, he must have had enough experience of loneliness, those days weeks that have to be forgotten, made up for somehow (how was she to decide), to understand loneliness although there was no comparison in kind . . . childhood is another state.

He said nothing, met her eyes for slow moments; the hold twitched away and his head stirred in what could be a questioning or assent.

Anyway. —I'm not using—taking anything.— It was up to nature to decide.

Berenice had no doubt of her fecundity. Most of her sexual life had been focused on avoiding it. But months went by and there was no conception. Blood every twenty-eight days. Was she prematurely ageing—at thirty-two, ridiculous. She had announced to her close colleagues that they'd have to find a temporary executive-level replacement at her desk, her computer, her conference telephone, for some months soon, she and her man had decided to have a second child. Now she confided it didn't seem to be happening. She took their experienced advice. It's nothing a gynaecologist can't prescribe for. The tests for fertility showed normal ovulation. On the prescription of the gynaecologist she instructed Paul and herself in what she called 'acrobatics', and intense frequency of lovemaking during fertile periods indicated by a rise in temperature she was to measure in her vagina. Strangely—unexpectedly in a male who had recently survived terminality—this vigorous frequent call on his sexual potency did not seem to affect him. When she alerted him in the wilderness over the radio contact (mobiles do not work too remotely from any power source) that the fertile period was warm in her, he came home to serve, and then to return to his wilderness.

There was still no conception. She consulted the gynaecologist again.

You ovulate all right, that's established. Your husband should have a sperm count.

Paul is to make an appointment with his doctor.

When is it?

He has not made an appointment.

Shall I give a call?

No, I'll do it.

He doesn't. Berenice/Benni stops asking.

Cannot.

Cannot submit himself, this self, to more tests, more procedures invading, monitoring his body. It performs, the penis is eveready, at hand, when he wakes in the morning, it gives and takes excitement when called upon, so frequently, to enter and empty itself to her in spurts of pleasure. Without reason, without any means of knowing by all the tests a laboratory trusts, without knowing if there could be any such reason, he half-believes the roving cells perhaps have not given up, the radiance that pursued to kill them keeps a pilot light somewhere low within him. His sperm may carry this. What kind of child could come of it.

He cannot trust his body. It remains the stranger that was made of it.

After some months of the good enough quality of the ordinary life that is valued only when it has been destroyed and then in some effort put together again—she has been made deputy director of the advertising agency, he has completed his on-location report on the Okavango for his team to place before the Minister of Environmental Affairs and release to the press—she brings up the subject of the second child. Not reproachfully, almost with a kind of hesitant tenderness?

—If you want another child you'll have to find another man.—

iv / *Get a Life*

Lyndsay didn't expect to be met at the airport. Paul was in Pretoria that day with a delegation of the World Conservation Union to the Minister of Environmental Affairs and it wasn't in any way Benni's obligation, indispensable to her clients as she was—advertising is a very personal transaction. But the mother had dinner with the son and his little family the evening of her arrival and Lyndsay and Paul spent time often, for one mutually-found reason or another, together while Adrian was away. Lunch when Paul found himself at his city offices, a walk with her on a Sunday (his suggestion, unexpectedly thoughtful, he certainly would have more interesting things to do). They carried something unexpressed between them. He didn't go to see her at the old house. She didn't ask him to. They had lived another time, another country, in common rather than actually together; it was not such an intimacy, elsewhere. They both, however, shared a sense of the rightness of Adrian having his chanced archaeological venture, the justice of the recognition of an avocation by the civil rights lawyer and the ecologist who had achieved their vocations. They'd never talked of this, but now that so many situations had come about that should never have been, in the home where he had been a child, she was able to reflect to him, with some questioning acceptance, how his father, her man, had given up the intention to be an archaeologist—at least until a time that never came. To dig into the prehistoric past didn't look likely to provide for the home-and-family contracted in marriage.

—Even though you were a working woman, a lawyer? Able to contribute? Must have been some other reason, in my father, that he couldn't—didn't want—

—I was a struggling beginner! A junior way down on the legal profession ladder, earning a clerk's salary. Not everyone *wants* as single-mindedly, absolutely as you do, has—what is it—all right, a calling that's significant of general survival and comes first, to be followed before everything, everyone, all else. Hardly anybody has the luck.— She looked away for a moment as if something had been forgotten. Smiled. —Or the loss.—

Was he a poor family-man, that what she meant. But the three words dropped away. What had emanated from him, isolated as a threat to others, means that the usual standards, rewards and punishments should not be applicable, so soon, to *him*. She read out from a letter she'd had a mishap related humorously, exasperation become a good story, from his father. A car the usually trusty Norwegian had hired suddenly began to behave like one of the volcanoes, smoking wildly, and the guide and her charge had to leave it burning itself out while they spent a night sitting up in the single-room adobe house of Indians with whom even the Norwegian linguist couldn't communicate. Not to worry, help came in the form of a passing bus next morning. He was sensibly staying on in the country a few days longer than the date he was expected home because the incident had wrecked not only the car but the trip to a site he most wanted of all to see, and who knows when he'd ever get the chance again. There followed a description of what he sought, was dug up there, which Lyndsay handed over to be read by Paul himself. —Sounds wonderful. I know the feeling, when we're out in the bundu and can't get to where we should be.—

The letter was warmth between them. She spoke of the third who belonged in it. —Really finding himself. I can see us having to pay a return visit.—

Three days before the date of his delayed arrival—she had saved and stacked in his retreat newspapers and journals of particular interest that he'd missed—she came with another letter. Paul was at home with Nickie, his opponent in some electronic game. After a few minutes as spectator she oddly asked her son if she could be alone with him. She spoke as if she could not believe what she heard herself saying. But the strangeness couldn't be questioned; an emanation, this time from her. He bribed the child to go to the care of the nanny (politically-correct: child-minder). The boy loved the woman, a cousin supplied by Primrose, and, without being aware of it, was learning to speak Setswana with her; a new generation that might produce white multilinguists, if not quite up to the level of Thapelo. The father grinned with pleasure, each time, to hear the little boy's few words.

Paul first stood a moment in front of his mother; then sat down not beside her, but in a chair, not far apart.

If anybody could have understood, it should have been she.

But when she unfolded the flimsy pages of handwriting as definitive as the features of the—Adrian's—face familiar to her as her own encountered in a mirror—ready for another account of the pleasures of his ancient discoveries, she did not understand what she was reading. She actually moved away the hand that was holding the letter, a moment, and then read again the first paragraphs. He wanted to be direct and honest with her, as he'd always been. Anything else would not be worth the value of their life together. Long life, including the indescribable recent experience in the house with their son. Long throughout her so deservedly successful career, his pride in it that would never change, and long through his working years to his retirement.

He found himself in love with the Norwegian girl. Woman really, she was nearly thirty-five. 'I am sixty-five. I had never imagined this could happen, not alone to me but to anyone this age, I'm a grandfather, for God's sake, I know, my working life is over. How can this begin again. I know you won't be able to believe it. I can't. But darling Lyn, it *is*. It's happened to Hilde and me. Thirty years between us. She was divorced from an Argentinian living in Mexico some years back, she's never had a child. And now she loves an old man who is somebody else's husband. I can't tell you how awful she feels about you, she liked you so much, we all got on well. So nobody wanted this to happen but it has, it has.

'We've suddenly been having what should be, I suppose, an affair. Holiday affair. I know, I know, old man's last fling. It seems I don't have flings; I fell in love with you and that was all I needed. For a lifetime as one has a life's work. Now I love this woman and can't deny it.

'What will happen I don't know. Although that's not the truth, I do know that I'm going to stay here in Mexico, with her, for the present.

'What's going to happen to us — you'll be asking as you read. I don't know. Only that I can't go on living in this state, behind your back, out of sight in Mexico. Of all places. It's had to happen in Mexico, where I've been able to follow the dream of anyone interested in archaeology to get to sites you've only read about. Through my bringing up the names of old *aficionados*, amateurs I've known, and some of the great discoverers like Tobias; and others, Wadley, Parkington and young Poggenpoel. I've even been able to spend a day sifting the dust on a current dig. Isn't that enough.

'It isn't. I can't lie.

'I can't say now, when I'll be coming back. To arrange things, whatever that may mean, for us to sit down and talk about this.

'No way to think of, to end the letter, for you.'
Just the signature, Adrian.

I thought you were going to tell me you were leaving.

He doesn't mention what else happened, what took away
four years of the lifetime of loving me. He's not forgotten,
ageing can't be as kind as that, he's wanting to make clear
there is no claim of justification, never mind revenge, in what
he's doing. Not true, for him or me or anyone, that this 'happens'; there is readiness for it and will, in entering it, the
state, even though it is alienation while it is fulfilment. It
doesn't 'happen' the way what happened to our son did. You
have to have known disaster to know the difference.

You are telling me you are leaving me.

She had to go to someone, take this second letter to be
verified in someone else's eyes, decoded independently. Not
information—family news—to give over a call to Emma in
Brazil. Or take to Jacqueline in her suburb north of the city,
or the resort of boarding a plane and going to Susan. Although none of the adult children knows of the mother who
was competent (not like Adrian's honest inability) to lie for
four years, the only one she can approach is the one who came
back in awful radiance to shelter in the childhood home. The
shared knowledge of the unspeakable makes it possible to
speak together of what is a banal disruption of intimate life.

With this son it can be as if it were not the situation of his parents: a certain objectivity she can count on because of the remove, even from those who risked occupying the same house, at which he lived for a period. It's in her nature as a lawyer, what else is there to place trust in, if not objectivity; truth—that's a matter far beyond. The judge declares it while it exists—escaped.

Yet it will be difficult, full of silences, to talk even to this son while she knows about the four years she lost for herself and his father. So the lie is back in the present. Lying once begun never ends.

She hopes, again, to find him alone. Imagine the embarrassment—or sophisticated lack of it—of Benni. Elderly men fall for women who could be their daughters, every day, maybe (interesting?) it could be repressed incest having a late try. Female sympathy would be forthcoming, you know how men are, while it's always been evident Benni can have no such complaint against hers, handsome and unusual a man as he must seem to other women.

One cannot be sure Benni/Berenice won't be there. She thought of calling. Might gather indirectly whether he was likely to be alone. He was back from one of his research assignments. She had learnt, when she took the couple to try with her a new Indian restaurant the week before, that he was having consultations about how best to take advantage of the extended deadline for objection to the Pondoland toll highway. He responded to her enquiry about how consultations were going and then mentioned he and Nicholas were a couple of bachelors, Benni away launching a wine festival at the Cape.

Could she come round? Of course. What about tomorrow, supper. But he at once acceded when she said couldn't it be today, this evening. He thought he should ask, are you all right—something must be bothering her. I'm all right. They were not two people who needed to or would press further on the tightrope of a telephone wire.

His mother put her palm over her mouth.

He waited for her—apparently to recover herself. It's an ambiguous gesture, it can hide laughter, shock, many conditions incapable of being conveyed. Embarrassment. But she was not embarrassed. Too many simple intimacies brought about by the incapacities of illness had existed between them for either to be embarrassed by anything, since.

—This has come from Adrian.—

He took the letter. Almost to himself, frowning in reproach —He hasn't gone and fallen down in one of his digs . . .—

She did not allow herself to look at the son's face as he read, slowly turning the two pages, and turning back to the first, as she had, to read again. If she has her habits of careful comprehension as a lawyer, as a student of scientific data in relation to experience on the ground he has his instinctive discipline of reassessing what are presented as the facts.

He could not say to her what was ready on his tongue: I thought he'd broken a leg or something, after all, nearly sixty-six, isn't he, climbing about in excavations. But no doubt, like himself, a young man accustomed to taking chances in difficult terrain, that would have been something she could have expected might catch up with retirement age.

The real circumstance made it impossible for the son to be (what she had counted on) objective; she became primary, there in front of him, his mother, threatened by that other primary, his father. He tried: retreated from the instinct to get up and embrace, make her, let her cry, and asked about the woman. As if his mother could find support in the familiar procedures of the court. Evidence.

—This's the woman you hired to go around with you, the guide you wrote was so excellent, not the usual boring windbag, not intrusive?—

—Yes. She was that.—

Not giving any come-on. To an old man. But he did not ask.

—The Norwegian.—

—The Norwegian. She was tactful, naturally we expected to have meals and so on with her along, but sometimes she would make it clear—some excuse, telephone calls, reminders of a private life somewhere—that she'd understand we'd want to be by ourselves, say, for dinner.—

From the father's, Adrian's side, what would be the attraction. First, what type of woman, what does she look like. —Is she pretty, beautiful, I mean what is there about . . .—

—How can I say. I'm a woman. I don't see what a man sees, you might see. Dark-haired, shapely plump but only in the right places, very intelligent. There's something I never understand, she has all the time that smile, the archaic smile that's characteristic of those ancient Greek statues, you know, the young men—what are they called, Khouroi? Adrian and I saw them once in Athens. Or was it a Roman museum. Even when the three of us rested somewhere with our eyes closed against the glare, stretched out on our chairs, whenever I happened to open my eyes there was this smile. Closed eyes, smile.—

—Irritating.—

—No. I thought it rather enviable, really. If I'd had to earn my living taking strangers about repeating the same information and listening to the same comments—what's a new way to say beautiful, disappointing—I don't think I could maintain that smile. And it was discreet.—

—And Adrian?—

—What about Adrian.—

—Did he ever say—anything—about her?—

—You know how he would naturally remark on the beauty of a woman, someone among our friends or yours we'd met. But I don't think he saw her as a beautiful woman. He would have said something . . . when we talked of what luck it was we'd found a Scandinavian, typically competent and friendly but keeping a distance.—

And now Lyndsay did not smile but gave a burst of breath, cutting herself off.

He still held the letter and began to skim it again, while half-handing it back to her.

Neither of them wanted it; it lay on the low table where the child's game was set out.

—So that's all changed. Just in the time they went off to-gether? The car and the adobe hut. Two weeks?—

—A few days more. I was going to meet him at the airport this coming Saturday, his postponed date to come home.—

—Ma (he reverted to the childhood address, once grown up he and his sisters, most often, called their parents as the parents preferred, by their names) . . . Ma, what are you think-ing of doing.—

She said nothing and neither did he. The lively frolic of

an exchange between Nickie and Primrose's cousin sounded from the kitchen.

—I've come to you.—

—But I can't know how you feel. He's my father, that's not the husband, the man, your man.—

—Are you angry with him.— As his mother's son.

—I suppose I am. Of course you are.—

—No, no, not angry. No right to be angry.—

If she had said something that might lead to doubts about his mother's own record, she quickly covered with a succeeding generalisation. —We don't own one another. Men and women don't.— If there's no barnyard hen there's no barnyard rooster.

No embarrassment to say (as if the father were dead) —He's always loved you so much. Any of us could see it. And so I suppose you . . . Sometimes we could be quite jealous.—

She would not know whether it was when 'we' were children (not loved enough) or whether he was contrasting his own life with a woman.

Look, this isn't the unbelievable of someone radiant with emanating danger, it's an ordinary human situation, if painful. Clear from the letter the one who loves once too often is in pain, too, although he can bury it in the body of his Norwegian. Lyndsay is a lawyer and lawyers' vocation is to deal with everything that has a legal status between birth and death. Rights. Lyndsay can divorce Adrian if she wishes, she has the conventional grounds, she knows exactly how you go about it although she's long left that level of legal practice behind for the higher ones of civil rights and constitutional law. Or she can leave him to pursue this *given* phase (love, sexual imperative is always a given), unplanned for retirement; wait. He doesn't seem to want, to be considering, a divorce, finality, in that letter. It's some sort of appeal— for what?

The mother and son understand this without discussion.

It is too soon, too raw, to receive the different answers there must be. And that's really the mother's necessity, the choices can't be of the same preoccupation, inevitability, to the son. He has left home, twice. He has his own life to live: that convenient cop-out of other intimate responsibilities. The generations can't help each other, in the existential affront. They are no closer than his awkwardness in a chair, might have been about to embrace her but clatter means the pair from the kitchen are bursting in upon them.

Lyndsay. Lyn. He's always loved you so much. The son could bring himself to witness that, not the kind of thing one says to a mother. Out of a soap opera, but not when it comes from him. He doesn't watch soap operas he reads trees and watercourses.

She does not reply to the letter at once. Reply? What does that imply. This happens and you do that. She did not call the hotel in Mexico City; perhaps he was expecting her to. Voice to voice if not face to face. She gave herself time, which was, supposedly, giving him time. To come home and say, as she knows one could, The affair's over. Weeping, as she had been. Whether for its end or for the betrayal it was of being loved so much. The more days she let go by before writing the letter that formulated and reformulated—crossed out, abandoned, and coming again into her mind (only in court, allowed no distraction, ever, did what he had made happen to her have no place), the more he would feel that he had her acquiescence, some sort of acceptance, her understanding he could not make a decision just as she could not, beyond his writing in his letter that for the time being he was simply staying on, visiting sites with his lover.

The longer the letter in return was unwritten, rewritten when she came home from Chambers to the old house that had never echoed empty on occasions when he was away and would be back on this day or that; when she lay in the dark and his side of the bed was flat, no body-horizon to be made out, the interpretation of what had come about was different. Life-work. All his life he had worked not grudgingly or unhappily, it appeared, with the satisfaction of doing what he had to do, conscientiously, in activity he wouldn't have chosen. The only culmination: retirement. The experience close to if not exactly fulfilment of his avocation (there's that mention he'd 'sifted the dust' that yields the past on an archaeological site), wasn't that enhanced by the realisation that there is another avocation, to love again. They go together. The woman and the archaeology. The lovemaking and the digs.

Perhaps this should be the contents of the letter, final draft before it got written. She did not think she could put it to the son, not even him. Even he would take it thankfully as a rationalisation. Rationalisation being essential in any solution for his mother. At least he would be too preoccupied, as he should be, with the remaking of his own life, to see how the rationalisation sifted through the familiar, familial dust to show everything of what the life of those two, parents, had been. Ordinary. A version of it. Just as his taking up again his wife/child/containing house—the elements of home— seemed to be reassembled.

The written letter was not any one of the unwritten drafts

with their flourishes of emotion, contradictions of cruelty (who would have thought you'd make a fool of yourself pushing seventy) and sad understanding (it's still good together, yes, even in bed).

Honest. To be the way he was.

I can't tell you I am anything but almost disbelieving, amazed. Because I've noticed, oh over all our years, even since you've been getting old, women having an eye for you, but Hilde didn't give any sign whatever of responding to you any more than she did to me. The same smile. And you—do I stupidly think people, the man and the woman, know each other so well after all those years that there couldn't be a change going on in one without the other sensing it. Apparently I did, do, think so. While we were together with the guide she was just that, smiling. You were just attentive, as I was, to the vivacious precision of her guidance to places and objects we wanted to see, and her knowledge of their history and meaning. No gallantry towards her—you know what I mean. In fact I thought you were relieved, in a way, when she excused herself from eating with us, we've never been at a loss for something we want to exchange over a meal alone. Perhaps I misread you, the strain of hiding the responses you were beginning to feel to her meant it was a relief for her not to be around for a while.

I suppose I should feel some reproach of her. But I won't. And there's no point, for her or for me, in her feeling 'bad'. As you write, it's happened, you both made it happen. From the letter it seems you don't know what you want (blocked out 'except not me') at present. So let it be an extended holiday, for now. I have shown your letter to Paul but for the girls the extended holiday will be the only explanation why you haven't come back, you're following more archaeological digs. The awkwardness that may result, if Emma gets to know you're lingering in Central America she'll want to persuade you to hop over to Brazil and see our grandchildren. ('Grand-children'. Was that cruel; but she left the ambiguous reference, did not cross it out.)

The letter was typed on her word processor. When she took up the copy, she had ready to write in her own hand, I love you. She wrote only the version of her name by which he knew her, Lyn.

It was unnecessary to warn Paul not to tell his sisters about the nature of the extended archaeological holiday. There was not much contact with them, anyway; family occasions of Christmas and New Year were long over and the social life arranged by Benni was peopled by her advertising colleagues now drawn together with some of his bushboys. Since he was no longer in quarantine, his affectionate sister Emma hadn't emailed from Brazil; presuming he didn't need her wild, amusing messages any more. Often it was Benni who would suggest his mother should come to dinner, and Lyndsay would arrive with a bottle of good wine. Benni would dutifully also ask, what news of Adrian, and appeared to listen as innocently as she did when Lyndsay told of some wonderful region he'd just driven through, adding —You two really must go to Mexico one day, it's dramatic. Worth the trip for the Museum of Anthropology alone.— If this was an interregnum his mother was managing it just as she had managed the isolation of quarantine.

She and her son have again something in common, as there was unknown to each in his reversion to childhood and her matching reversion, then, of reliving the shame of four lollipop years. They have each the dedication beyond the personally intimate, of belonging to the condition of the world. Justice. The survival of nature. Whatever the condition of their intimate lives, she was fully committed with her colleagues to the complexities, the apparent dead ends to be followed and disproved, the nuance of statements to be deciphered, the lies to be disentangled from facts, in the corruption cases for which they were briefed, and which certainly would go on, with adjournments and referrals, for months. Another extended period. And he, with Thapelo and Derek, was back and forth to the coastal dunes, now, of the Eastern Cape, where the government's decision to allow mining for titanium and other metals was pending—same area as the toll highway project. The subject of begetting another child, companion for Nickie, had not come up again. What he had said, that time, put an end to it. They made love when he was home from the dunes, smelling, she told him, of the sea; which roused her, evidently. He assumed she had protected herself against insemination. Protected herself from Him.

His mother became somehow part of the life returned to, taken up, in his house; as if with the end of its occupation as a place of quarantine and in the absence of the father, the old house was no longer home. She was quite often found with Nicholas and Benni, when he came back to the city, to his life there. Seems she had some sort of relationship, if not close at least comfortable, to the combination personality Berenice/ Benni with whom she had little in common. Well—himself and the boy. As the archaeological holiday, the fulfilment of

an avocation long denied—that was how it came to be un-
spokenly accepted—indeed extended it took on something of
the established ordinariness that had been achieved by Lyndsay in the period of a quarantine. Apparently she filled her
time in the company of other women rather than the married couples who were her friends and Adrian's. Her son supposed this was usual with women not looking for a new man,
or disadvantaged by age or a sense of distaste for such a pursuit; not something he would have given a thought to if it
hadn't been out of concern about his mother. Apart from the
parents' circle of mutual friends, she had tended to have hers
among the legal fraternity—fraternity, yes, because most
judges and prominent lawyers were male. She brought to
lunch one Sunday what it is clear was a particular new friend,
not a lawyer but a social worker, and not a nice middle-class
do-gooder like the ones who might be among the married couples, but a woman employee of the local government Social
Welfare department. She was coloured, one in whose broad
face, a composite image of the Khoi Khoi, San, Malay, Dutch,
English, German and only the past knows what else, was
pleasingly mixed. She was presented as Charlene-Somebody
but cut in with a laugh, Just call me Charlene, that's me.

Lyndsay defined, in dismissal of modesty —She's been
introducing me to the realities my colleagues and I only see
as the end result. She took me yesterday to a hospice, no, I
suppose you'd call it a half-way home for babies. Abandoned
babies, some of them HIV-infected or already with AIDS.—

—Ghastly thought. That must have been hard to take.—
Benni, like Adrian, is also honest, coming out with the crude
reaction others would suppress in order not to appear to lack
human feeling.

This Charlene sensed some explanation was appropriate for how the introduction to a reality came about, and also perhaps unable to suppress an impulse to show her quality in becoming mentor to someone in a high position of the authoritarian world. —Ag, you see, I've just been a witness in that big case, you know, my brother-in-law who was kicked out of his firm, his job, he was assistant manager in a supermarket, because he's got AIDS—how he got it, that's another story, not for me—the trade union made a case to defend him and Mrs Bannerman was the chief lawyer—

—Unlawful dismissal. We won. It's something of a test case with implication for others. Charlene Damons was an outstandingly good witness—the attorney who was supposed to prepare her said it was the other way about—

The two women laughed; this testimony must have been what led Lyndsay to take an interest in the woman. Obviously initiated some opportunity to talk to her; time has long passed when coffee shops were segregated and there was nowhere to go. Over the Sunday lunch Lyndsay encouraged voluble Charlene, who didn't need much urging while she composedly enjoyed her food and the usual wine the host's mother contributed, to tell about her work among people suffering HIV and AIDS, in particular workers employed in industry and chain stores.

—What happens to the babies? Many die? And if they survive, with treatment. They do get treatment?— Benni is wiping the traces of icecream from round Nickie's mouth.

—Many die. What can you do. They've been left in public toilets. Some in the street, the police find them and bring them in.—

—The mothers?—

—Nobody knows the mothers, who're the fathers.—

Lyndsay has been turned away, listening. —But when you see them, their faces. They look like someone. Not nobody.—

There's proof. Nickie, icecream-besmeared face, looking like—Paul, Benni, Lyndsay. Adrian. And progenitors farther back. As the elements that converge in the Okavango; as the natural forces of alchemy create the sand dunes secreting minerals from still earlier formations.

The new kind of family lunch passed uneventfully enough with the guest; Paul and Benni didn't encounter her again. Lyndsay was engaged in a new case, her next offering was not an individual but a letter, first of several, read out to the family as sometimes she brought along an email from Emma; a letter from Adrian telling something of whatever it was that he was living. A state awkward to categorise. Travels to the mountains, natal region of Zapata, more Rivera paint ings seen, the weather. Archaeological excavations, of course. In one letter, he said he was thinking of writing something. The experience of seeing these unearthed accomplishments of the ancient past when you belong to an era where there are wars going on over who possesses weapons that could destroy all trace of it. (The letters were addressed like publicity leaflets headed 'The Occupier', 'Dear family' on the first page.) When Lyndsay came to these few sentences her distanced tone sounded to the others a sign that they were meant for her alone.

She probably wrote back—would she?—the same kind of letters with matters skimmed from the surface of what the family was living; whether there were words, residue of the exchanges of the personal, not the ancient, past, coming pri- vately from her to him was her own affair, her son couldn't speculate any more than he could foresee any resolution the parents might come to for themselves.

The government's announced project for a Pondoland 'marine protected area' wasn't going to be any resolution for the sand dunes on that coast. It protected the waters alone. The Australian-based Mineral Commodities could still go ahead with their plan to mine twenty kilometres of the dunes. With Thapelo and Derek surrounded by a paper-territory of surveyors' maps and their own field notes, the team sat with representatives from Earthlife Africa and the Wildlife and Environmental Society following the trail of contradictory statements, a palimpsest over what was before them.

—The Minister's passing the buck. Just listen again. Environmental Affairs: 'The Minister remains opposed to the mining and instead supports ecotourism in the area. But ultimately the decision to mine on the Wild Coast rests with the Minister of Minerals and Energy.' *Ja-nee.*— Derek's jerks of the head mimic 'yes-no'.

—The Mineral Commodities outfit must have submitted for the Aussies the application to Minerals and Energy by now. Department's sitting on it. While that's going on and Mineral Commodities' spin doctors are lobbying, you can depend on that, we've got to keep pushing, man, pushing. They're going over the Pondoland Marine Park projects, they say, to 'assess' how it will affect their mining plans, but that's nonsense, shaya-shaya, their chief exec's already said the frontal dune and riverine systems had always been excluded from the mining areas—they're not— Thapelo hoists the flag of one of the surveyors' maps.

A heat of frustration rises with it. Paul waves a hand up across the table as if clearing this emanation. —Lobbying—

that's only part of the strategy. Bribery is going to serve them even better. The option they've given to a black empowerment company that represents the very community, the traditional leaders we counted on, the people *we've* been lobbying to protest misuse of their land, threat to their subsistence. A fifteen percent stake in the mining deal, ten million dollars. Ten million! How does that divide up among—how many people? It doesn't; going to be shares on the stock exchange. Doesn't matter. It's a sum that fills the sky.— His rolling glance tilts inadvertently at Thapelo, who shouldn't be singled out; wanting the empowerment of money is a characteristic of whites as well, at least human temptation isn't discriminatory. The difference is whites have held that power exclusively, so long. —How does that look for protest against the toll road that's going to break up their habitat, the mining that's set to destroy the dunes there? So? We don't want rural blacks to have a share in the growth of economic power? It's not for them? They're out of the mix in our mixed economy? What're we going to say to that.—

Thapelo slaps his hands across his chest to strike and grab his biceps. —We have to live with it, Bra. Race sensitivity's out, my man, for this thing. Those big money boys know how to operate rings round us. For sure there's a link, a deal, between the toll highway and the mining, let the Mineral Commodities set-up and the government deny it, shout from now till tomorrow, you saw how the National Road Agency says the road will reduce transport costs, that's important for the products of the mine, getting the stuff to the smelter.—

—And finally to the stock exchanges of the world.—

—And the ten million dollar shareholders scattered by the highway. Who'll get the dividends.—

—The makhosi.—

Paul turned from the contest of words to decisions. —We're only a couple of months before the deadline for final objections to the mining project. Co-ordinate all the organisations and groups for action, jack up overseas support (Berenice's vocabulary comes in useful, an unfamiliar weapon). Get a life, man!—Let's make up and bring a high-profile party of save-the-earthers to come as observers of what's at stake— not the low-voltage ones we've had—some pop stars who'll compose songs for us, *Come rap for the planet*, prove they're good world citizens . . . it's cool now for the famous to take up causes—

—Right on, my brother!—

Maybe her advertising agency would know exactly how to manipulate this, now desperately become like any other publicity campaign.

Lyndsay had left a message among those waiting on his mobile phone. Responding to relevant others, he forgot about it. She called again—it's just to say she'd like to come round this evening, if he and Benni were going to be home, hadn't seen them for a week. Yes, eat with us. No, she'd come for coffee. You know we don't drink coffee after dinner, Ma, and neither do you. Laughter. For a drink then, fine.

His mother arrived after nine without acknowledgement of being later than expected and with the air of having pleasantly concluded some preoccupation. Benni, in the worldly sophistication of Berenice, even tolerantly wondered to herself whether Lyndsay hadn't found some man attracted to her, she still looks good despite her age; it can happen. Mother and son had a glass of wine, Benni for some reason puts her hand over the glass Paul has put beside her. Must be some new diet she's put herself on, well-promoted . . . There's Danish aquavit in the cupboard, which she favours, but the Scandinavian association is perhaps not tactful.

—I've been meaning to tell you for some weeks but there have been legal complications, still are . . . no point in waiting for that to be final. You remember, I brought a welfare worker, witness in one of my cases, along to lunch. Someone who'd taken me to see abandoned babies—children in a home. Well, I went back there on my own a few . . . a number of times. I felt, I don't know, there was a child, a small girl, she's about three the paediatrician says, one can't be exact with an abandoned child, she responded to my turning up— presence. She was brought in by the police seven months ago, that means she was about two years old, then. She'd been raped and she's HIV-positive. She had to be (Lyndsay, always professionally, unhesitatingly precise—hands up—at a loss how to define this for others) . . . reconstructed . . . surgery . . . weeks in the children's hospital. Apparently it was successful, far as they can tell with a female so young. Then she was handed back to the institution. They're happy—the people in charge at that place—if they think you're trustworthy, you want to give one of the inmates—kids—a treat, an outing. So I took her to the zoo, you must introduce Nickie to the baby seal that's just been born— she was ecstastic. I've decided she couldn't go on living in an institution, good though it is. There are very few adoptions of HIV-positive children. The home has released her already. She's with me. I'm adopting her.—

—What have you done.— He has stumbled into some place in Lyndsay's life closed against him. Can't see her there.

—I'm finding out. Quite an experience.— She raises eyebrows, serene. —You can imagine how delighted Primrose is. She's in charge while I'm in Chambers and court.—

His mother gives time for silence, for Paul and Benni/ Berenice to accept what is done. Her son is with her in quarantine in the garden, they are statues, commemorating their habitation there. —How will Adrian. What about Adrian?—

She is alone with Paul, since the quarantine there will always be this facility, apart from the presence of others.

The words flung down before him.

—What about Adrian.—

She went back to that babies' shelter, one Saturday when she had walked past a toy shop in a mall and been beckoned by a display of anthropomorphic bears, monkeys and leopards dressed in jeans. Nickie had pillow-mates like these; there was a jungle gym she'd noticed the unidentified children climbing when she accompanied her outstanding witness to their reality, but were there any toys like these, personal treasures. She bought a few, and went to drop them off in the rundown quarter of the city where the institution was. Those inmates old enough to walk or at least sit were having their supper at tables right for their size. A small girl she recognised from the first visit jumped up, overturning some mess in her plate, and came running, to the toys, not the woman; she took her time, gazed at the bear, the leopard, the monkey, and carefully chose the monkey. Others clamoured round.

Was it foolish to bring a few luxury toys where there were—how many had Charlene said—thirty or more babies and children, the number went up and down as some died and one or two, healthy ones, might be adopted. Would they quarrel over possession—the recognised girl had run off with her monkey. Well-meaning could be mistaken.

She returned a week later, not with gifts that might obviously cause trouble, maybe create a contentious privilege, difficult to imagine a child who doesn't have any, in the democracy necessary in such a place—to ask if she could take the claimant of the monkey to the zoo to see real ones. The girl had been in care for months, she was told, found without a name, not old enough to know if she did have one, the staff called her Klara. Getting to know the features that made the child whoever it was, she was (couldn't be expressed to oneself less clumsily) proposed the wonderful mystery of the personality, how it may be signalled in the set of the nose, the shifting line of lips in speech (this little creature talks a lot, an incoherent coherence of whatever African language she had shaped when she learnt to speak and the English she had learnt to obey from the whites among the Salvation Army people whose institution cared for her). Here was a small being creating herself. The distinguished-looking woman, maybe a politician or something, who came back after Charlene brought her, became well-known to the Army's female Major and was allowed to take lucky Klara away for weekends, then was listed a foster-parent, Klara officially in her care. A bed, a place vacant for another, born not in a manger but a public toilet. Better not ask what next for the small girl if the lady tired of her. Because Lyndsay, also, did not know what next. For herself; for the child; in the meantime she did not make her guest? charge? known to Paul and his family.

Her own motives were suspect to her. Then they were of no concern, she and this stranger with a vividly distinct self,

stranger no more, had a life in common. A nursery school accepted her, dropped off there every morning by Lyndsay on
the way to Chambers, and Primrose kept her fluent in a
mother tongue in the afternoons. Lyndsay did mention to a
colleague that she was taking care of someone's black child;
it was not the sort of temporary situation without precedent
in the individual social conscience of their legal practice—at
least had not been during the apartheid years when clients
defended on charges of treason sometimes had no choice but
to leave a child abandoned. There was a good chance, said
the paediatrician Lyndsay took the child to, that her HIV-
positive status would correct itself shortly; the blood count
was encouragingly mounting. This reprieve could happen
only in children. So there was an interim decision; don't look
further than that. She wrote one of the spaced letters she and
Adrian exchanged, like the form letters to aunts etc. taught
to phrase, at school, where she told that Paul was in a helicopter monitoring the terrible floods in the Okavango, and
related the progress of Nicholas swimming over-arm instead
of dog-paddling, beginning to count up to twenty-five, recognise words in story-books. (Relating to herself; Klara, able already to string red and white beads alternately on a cord, has
to be stopped from attempting to climb the jacaranda in the
garden, insists on mastering the use of a fork at the age of
about two-and-a-half or three.)

Enquiries, to someone who dealt with these things, about
the processes of adoption are routine in informing oneself
how the child might better be offered to someone where she
could grow up in the company of siblings, a father and mother.
There was no point she would really remember when instead
she had become the adoption applicant, informing herself.

The process is not simple, even in the case of a child of un-known parentage, abandoned no-one knows by whom. But it was the time to inform her son and his family.

Should Paul's mother be invited to bring along the child when she came to his house; where Nickie was? Lyndsay, that awesome lawyer rationalist (Berenice's one of the impover-ishers of their mother tongue who make the epithet as de-void of religious force as 'fuck' is devoid of force to shock), not only decides at her age and in her situation to adopt a small child but must have one who is infected with the Dis-ease. Does anyone honestly know whether or not it can be transmitted ways other than sexually or by blood? If by blood, what happens when two children play together and there are scratches, blood exchanged. Nickie's a boy, quite rough, if still small. Benni/Berenice—everything must be taken into consideration—decides to put a hold on such visits, tactfully, until Paul is home. She knows Lyndsay well enough, in the shift the plight of Adrian has somehow brought about, to think Lyndsay will understand, not comment upon to Paul.

—The child's accepted at a nursery school.— Paul's like his mother, depends on evidence, whether it's a conservation back-of-beyond or their private lives in question.

—Not all nursery schools. Wasn't there even a case—a woman went to court when a kid was refused. The nursery school pointed out that very young children bite when they get in a temper.—

—The child's how old?—

—It's not sure, about three. I suppose they tell by the

teeth and not all come out at the same rate. Nickie's were early.—

Benni was not particularly surprised, not confused as he was, he saw, when his mother came out with it just before he went to the drowned Okavango that now was the scene in un-obliterated vision, present after-image in his awareness. He could not place, with Lyndsay, this action. She had never been particularly fond of children, it seemed, kept a kind of privacy even between herself and the four she bore (had it been Adrian who wanted a family, and now left them to her) and she didn't drool and coo over her grandchildren although she and Nickie were rather companionable, he loved this special friend.

Benni appeared rather to be amused by his discomfiture. The wilderness is an innocent environment whatever else he exposes there; he doesn't know what goes on in the real world. Doesn't know it's become quite trendy to adopt a black child, or an orphan from, say, Sarajevo or India. She could tell him it proves something. But in Lyndsay's instance, she can't haz-ard what.

She sees he won't oppose—whatever Lyndsay decides, he is convinced is all right. For Nicholas: he doesn't decide, for Nicholas. She should, she wants—fuck him if he doesn't put his child first, above all the orphans in the world—to turn on him angrily but she does not. In this life put together since the time he went home again, out of touch, there is still, un-derneath, something between him and the woman who is his mother that shuts out everyone. He's here in the bedroom but the lines are down.

Whatever it is she wanted to prove by adopting in old age, and on her own, a child who might die and whose physical possibilities of growing up with the birthright of a female, clitoris, labia, and vagina, must be damaged however clever the surgery was, his mother's choice isn't an easy one. This bright and beguiling little girl is self-willed in excess of her size and approximate age, manipulative, a show-off in the spotlight of demanded attention and the next half-hour gloweringly withdrawn. —Just plain naughty.— The foster-mother/grandmother laughs even when exasperated.

Who knows if the virus covertly hunts this child down as rogue cells may still be holed up somewhere along his bloodstream. His mother is an old hand at interpreting prognosis, monitoring it coming about either in its negative or positive proof, back in the quarantine, his. And as then, she somehow establishes, creates ordinariness in this other unwelcome metamorphosis of a family—Adrian missing, some other being added—out of uncertainty, the unresolved. Which surely

you've learnt by example of ecological solutions, is a condition of existence? No? Is she compensating for lack, loss of
him, Adrian—is he coming back? Is she punishing Adrian by
showing she makes bolder choices than his, going all the way
to the exhibition (no less) of extreme moral choice, taking on
some child not orphaned but even worse, abandoned, and still
further from human to inhuman act, a victim raped, disease-
infected, while in the state of total innocence. Is his mother
showing off; as the showing-off, the rages, the defiance of the
flirtatious round-eyed, soft-mouthed near-baby is a punish-
ment of whoever conceived her, abandoned her, thrust and
tore open her body, planted a virus there.

Lyndsay takes Nickie and Klara to the zoo. Klara demands,
The sa-el, the sa-el, and Lyndsay corrects her. The two children raise a chant: *The see-al, the see-al!* Other visitors smile
at the little scene, assuaging pleasantly their guilt of the past
when the zoo was closed to blacks except on one day a week
and black and white children did not chant together.

Does his mother feel Adrian's eyes on her from somewhere in the fjord—wherever whatever—the stratosphere
that is his absence? Does he see these occasions of hers as
defiance?

Or isn't she thinking of Adrian at all, at the zoo with her
grandchild and her child. Not when she and Klara come to
the son's house at weekends—it's nice for Nickie to have a
playmate who is naturally part of the family. Adrian has left
Mexico. But not to come home. When they're at table together, the Paul-and-Benni table that has become the family
one now that Lyndsay doesn't set it at the old family home,
there is a dismissal of awareness that there is an empty chair.
Apparently it's a ruling that the father's, the individual

Adrian's choice be respected. Human rights exclude mawk-
ish sentimentality as useless while disguising that it is
painful is a better reason. He is in Norway with his sometime
guide. They live in Stavanger, one of the northern ventures
he and Lyndsay never made. Hilde has a sister there; I'm
occupying a flat in the old family house, I have a view of the
port. He writes in the first person singular, not 'we'. Of course
it must be that Lyndsay writes back at intervals that match
those of his letters; has she told him, does she write about
Klara; she will have told him that the Judicial Commission
has appointed her to the Bench. She is about to become a
judge. A son has to stop himself from blurting, He'd be so
proud of you—the licence of high emotions that allowed
him to tell her, He always loved you so much, was over.
Adrian is in Stavanger, taken retirement and presumably writing his thoughts on seeing—what was it—the dug-up accomplishments of ancient times while living in an era of
weapons that could destroy itself without trace.

Nickie and Klara get on well together in the contesting
manner of small children, she a tough match for the elder
and male. And when he retaliates by tugging at a vulnerable
attribute she has and he hasn't, her dreadlocks (Primrose insists on plaiting them to adorn a fashionable little black girl),
she squeals piteously for help as the playmate who when
pinned down on the grass had yelled that a gogga was biting him. Nothing further has been said between Paul and
Benni about the girl's HIV 'status', in fact that established
euphemism placed at a remove the remote possibility—
unproven?—that the contact of scratched knees could trans-
mit infection. Only when tussles between the two tumbling

and cavorting children become too intense, the no-escape moment when a boxer is forced against the ropes, both Paul and Benni rush, colliding to part them. Lyndsay keeps the girl's fingernails very short: whether for hygiene or a precaution to which she would not admit credibility.

All right, the zoo. City children learn of their existence—co-existence—with animals other than cats and dogs. When Nicholas is older, take him along on working assignments; it'll be some years, the conditions are not for small kids, but a youngster of eleven or twelve, that'll be the time. Children see something of the wider concept of the environment on television—does Benni really put the boy in front of nature programmes, as supposed, instead of the monster-hero sagas he takes as his spacemen toys come to life. That's not seeing, smelling the living creature in flesh and fur; at least a zoo provides that. But childhood doesn't provide only in a garden, signals to what is going to be decisive in adulthood. There's the extraordinary dark memory like those in nightmares, but not dispelled by morning, and time: the eagle, in that same zoo which is now his mother's treat for the next generation, hunched on claws within the stone walls and close roof of a cage. Something frightening in prescience of what would only be understood, known, shared years later: despair. The caged eagle become a metaphor for all forms of isolation, the ultimate in imprisonment. A zoo is prison.

Benni lifts and drops her shoulders, which stirs her breasts; kill-joy, not everyone can have the freedom of the wilderness and anyway he retreats into silence, some other place, when (again) she offers one of the clients' game parks, no cages there, foreigners fly thousands of miles to find marvellous. She has again suggested a stay, his mother and Klara included, this time, at one of the weekend breaks away from the city, Agency-featured, these beautiful half-wildernesses. All he says absently is that the children are too young to spend hours being driven around in a four-by-four. You need Japanese stamina for that. And so makes Benni laugh. Thank— what are their gods?—for the Japanese, they're the staples of our tourist industry!

There is a place where the eagle he has not forgotten, its species, is free. That's a near-by outing for the children, the family, owed by this father who too often is absent; in his wilderness.

The Black Eagle, *Aquila verreauxii*, has been breeding at this cliff above a waterfall since 1940. These highly territorial birds, with a weight of approximately five kilogrammes and a wingspan of up to 2.3 metres are one of Africa's largest and most majestic eagles. The Black Eagle pair in the Roodekrans territory can be seen all year round. They spend their days hunting, soaring, displaying, or perching on their favourite roosting spots, where they rest and preen. They live on the Rock Hyrax, hares, and guinea fowl. The breeding cycle commences in March/April, when one of the two nesting sites will be used in a specific breeding year. Sticks are placed to form a nest cup that will be completed with leafy twigs. This creates a soft lining in the cup prior to egg laying which normally occurs in May. The male performs spectacular courtship displays during the refurbishment. The pair mate for life and take a new mate only if one should die.

Paul read out from a leaflet picked up at the entrance to the park space, half botanical garden for indigenous African species, half wildlife protection habitat. The two small children neither listen nor understand, the information is for himself, Lyndsay and Benni, Nicholas and Klara are simply excited at the beginning of any excursion. Do they know what an eagle is? You're going to see a ve-ery big bird. Lyndsay attempted to make the excitement specific but the focus of the two for whom the world of nature is new was wide and low, there were gaudy butterflies to chase and Nickie spied a caterpillar articulated like the coaches of a toy train. Paul carefully lifted it from a leaf, opened the boy's hand and placed it gently in the palm, to protests from Berenice. But he addressed Benni, the boy's mother. He mustn't be taught to be afraid of everything that isn't human or domesticated. And if it happened to be a scorpion? That's part of the knowledge: learning to recognise what's harmful and what's not.

Life-skills—that's the term she would understand. And he doesn't expect—or want—anyone to understand that what he's been able to say simply, without his kind of jargon is— simply—the principle of what he does, it's called ecology.

Lyndsay turns out to know more about the strange sculptural plants than he. It used to be said of such growths that they're like something from the moon, but now it's known there is no growth on the moon, there's no comparison with nothingness. She is able to name substitutes for leaves like buttocks; an elephantine lump of grey as a desert species from Namibia which stores water in its bulk for nourishment during the long dry years. In the period when Namibian independence was being negotiated she had been there as part of a legal team and Sam Nujoma himself had arranged for her to be taken into the desert—not that Paul or his wife would know or is likely to remember who the first president of the country's sovereignty was.

From every experience, professional or otherwise, there's always some aspect detached from the whole. The negotiating process subsumed by the history-that-is-memory; the identity of some weird growth is there, available, named.

While the family outing straggles along the paths to the waterfall you can hear but not see: in the susurration, *I thought you were going to tell me you were leaving.*

(The children chasing about each other or the butterflies butt against adult thighs as if these were tree trunks.)

That's all that comes out of that state of existence, and why not; so definitive as it was at the time. And it did not happen, the leaving. Mate for life. The affair is over. Case closed; it has not been reopened for long years. And now quite differently—no, come on, admit it—the same, has been reopened. I am sixty-five I never imagined this could happen it's happened to Hilde and me. The child chosen as black, defiled, infected, nameless—something else that has happened. One of the states of existence. Paul is taking up each child in turn to be swung round him as he walks; the son has come out of quarantine and seems to be in possession of a new state.

They arrive suddenly at the sight of a swag of silver down

the dark of rock-face. The children did not appear to find it so striking, perhaps to them it was the bath water gushing from a giant tap. As they all drew nearer the cliff, rifted steeply in a narrow jagged cut beside the waterfall, rose to block the sky: *go no farther*. There was a grass plateau between bush-shaggy hills on either side, before the pool where the water fell and quietened. Now the plunge was white and in swift heavy strands, some leapt thinly to drop independently, chiffon of mist strayed, the water-voice volume turned up to an obliterating ringing in the ears. Klara danced with her hands over hers. Well it's not Niagara but it's pretty impressive. Benni appreciative, to Paul as if it was a spectacle he had created.

He must find the eagle. Flights of small birds scattered the sky above the cliff. He scanned the cliff again and again and discovered the two nests, if the haphazard collection of dry black twigs on ledges were nests. Benni had waited her turn at the telescope provided for visitors and reported the people around her confirmed these were the nests. While he was narrowing his focus on what seemed no more than garden detritus, his gaze was suddenly swivelled up and round by something that blocked out peripheral vision on the left. The eagle, not hunched way back in despair, the sail of a huge black wing glancing. He called out to the others, the mother, the wife, and in the stance of braced legs, head making an arc of his back, followed the flight, powerful enough to challenge the sky, of a scale to match it. The eagle, now a black cloak unfurled, now an immense black paper kite soaring, was in an arabesque with another, they were dipping and rising in great circles around the air up there, for a moment one of the spread wings actually blinded the sun as a man's

hand across his eyes can do. There was a flash of white when
the underside of this missile was revealed, but the plumaged
body, like the hook of the head, hardly made out, was of no
significance, the wings were the being of the creature's mastery. Lyndsay was the one who noticed leafy twigs, as the
leaflet had described, on the mess of the nest on the right—
from the viewer's not the bird's point of view. The wings of
night against sun-paled sky continued to plane and dip; and
then there was a descent, the transforming mastery that was
the eagle's was gone, collapsed in a bird. As it readied to land
on the nest that surely couldn't contain it, it seemed to gather
itself together, almost fold up, only head and beak erect. The
head had not mattered, in the air. Only the wings. They had
appeared to be directed only by the intelligence of their own
velocities, power over air and space. He inveigled himself
near the front of the small gathering at the telescope. A head
faced straight at him, drawn close by the glass. A flat dark
head holding the great black polished orbs that are eyes, ringed
with gold. These orbs separated by a broad white scimitar
ending in a black hook. A nose a beak—it's impossible to take
in the features of any face as a total vision—if this creature
has what could be called a face at all, it is received as a certain
feature of a face. (A woman's mouth, that's what he always
sees.) This being named eagle turns the head; in profile the
head hardly demarcated from the neck and the wide shoulders of the wings confirms the definition: the statement of
the curve of the nose-beak, sense-organ and weapon. How is
it that the high curved nose of Semitic people, the Jews and
Arabs, is despised as unaesthetic by other peoples, when it has
kinship across the species, with the magnificent eagle? Now
the folded, self-domesticated creation somehow settles itself

on its Procrustes' bed of twigs, some of them falling as the claws (noticed for the first time) extend and retract for a hold, and they, across species, are like the knobble-boned crenellated skin of very old human hands, although these retain powers which the hands never had.

Lyndsay has taken the children down to the low wooden barrier on the verge of the pool. Is the susurration louder or muffled by the overhang of the cliff and awareness of the crowding hills; it encloses her along with the imperceptible mist rather than comes through the ears. There was a dinner at the house of a judge whose colleague she is about to be, she was placed at table as unattached guests are beside another apparently unattached guest, in the male-female protocol. He is a retired judge from some other region of the country— she would hardly be partnered with somebody younger. The talk is of politics, the last elections and the President's appointment of a woman as Minister of Justice. If the man assumes that his neighbour welcomes the appointment because she is herself a woman, he is in for what no doubt will be a surprise. Her contribution to the comments in chorus above the plates and flower-piece: I'm celebrating the Minister not because she is a woman and so am I, but because she is exceptionally well qualified for the portfolio. If it had been a man with the same credentials, I'd be raising my glass to him. There was laughter and bravos from several of the men, and a glance-shaft of disapproval from a woman. But no-one could question the judge-elect's position on human rights.

Klara and Nicholas are shaking the slats of the barrier and have to be stopped. Klara's angry: Swim! Swim! A new word acquired along with the swimming lessons she was having in company with Nickie. There are two small boys flashing

darkly agile skinny legs, paddling at the edge of the water although there is a sign indicating that this is forbidden, a rule
ignored by the trio of women, two wearing the hijab, to whom
they belong. Hopeless to explain, even to Paul's son, that nothing must disturb this habitat. Klara's begun to collect leaves
and throw them at the pool, but always safely misses.

Probably it was the remark about the appointment of the
woman Minister that made him more interested in his dinner partner with whom he had engaged in casual exchange
before the subject animated the guests. Must have been told
she was about to go to the Bench—a hostly precaution against
the embarrassment of asking, And what do you do? He'd also
picked up something, one of those useful scraps that start a
conversation. And you're interested in archaeology, we all
need a break when on the Bench, I know too well. No, that
was her husband; and since the spouse wasn't in the place oc-
cupied by the retired judge, there was the casual explanation,
He's visiting sites in Mexico. The liveliness of the continuing
political discussion put an end to the subject.

It emerged easily that they held views of a judiciary in
their transformed country in common, with the intriguing
circumstance that he was viewing participation from his past
on the Bench under apartheid segregation law and she was
about to enter her appointment in a democracy. Seventy or a
year or two older, then; no attempt to draw remaining strands
of blond-grey hair across the bald head above a cliff forehead, tall and upright, looked still to have his own teeth. He
sat across other tables in the restaurants where there followed
invitations to dinner with him. Why not. He is a colleague
with interests in the theatre and art exhibitions apart from
his successfully concluded profession, no avocation, just the

pastime pleasures of a life. He speaks of his wife who died two years ago. She has found it honest in the openness that excludes familiarity, with someone her own kind, a colleague in law, to tell him that she is parted from Adrian Bannerman. He does not intrude any questions.

Now she hears from a friend that he wants to marry her. Only yesterday, in the course of a phone conversation with a woman for whom a call is a confession of her own intimate decisions and a preoccupation with those of others. The man 'is in love with her'. At his age, more than sixty-five, when it does, can happen. They have not gone to bed.

She picks up Klara, this circumstance of hers, happened, chosen, to distract the child, pointing out a big black bird balanced there on the rock.

Marry her. Do you become a virgin again, to an ageing man? That's why first there's a rumour as a preparation for the unexpected passionate kiss in place of the civilised goodnight peck between new friends, which she tolerated, come on—half-enjoyed—put down to the bottle of good wine finished over dinner. For him, not to be attributed to wine but as a show of confidence in his ability—still—as a lover. The idea of marriage a kind of delicacy, a prelude, because they are not young, to becoming lovers.

Klara struggles, she is not interested in something you can't grab for, far away.

The water is so loud you could almost shout against it without being heard. Not here in the nature conservation park or in Stavanger.

Middle-age folly—how old, in my forties. But our time after, and the last time whenever it was. Adrian.

The last man inside me.

Mate for life.
Klara slides free down that body.

His mother rejoined Paul who was reading out to his wife further information he had found in an array of pamphlets on a bench. Only two eggs, that's the entire clutch. It'll happen next month, June. The first egg laid hatches and is followed about a week later by a second. The two chicks, known as Cain and Abel. The first-born, Cain, has already grown when Abel comes out of his shell. Cain and Abel fight and generally Abel is killed by Cain and thrown from the nest. The survivor is fed by both parents until around December when it's able to fly . . . five years to reach adulthood and black plumage . . . time for the eagle to find its own mate and territory.

Cain and Abel. But what if one chick's a female—suppose you can't call one of these birds a hen.

Benni/Berenice is right. Lyndsay offers —She also gets kicked out, I suppose, it's a way of keeping the balance of nature, Paul? Neither too many nor too few males and females for breeding. But it's horrible.—

Leaning on the balustrade of rough steps hewn into the cliff, the language of the pamphlet in hand fails to represent the being of the withdrawn black entity on the bed of dead wood and the other disappearing off into the sky and returning in the guise of a menace or as deliverance of omniscience, as the surveyors' plans and the reports he writes fail to represent the Okavango or the Pondoland dunes. Oh this is not the smallness of man stuff, against nature. Romanticising what's too heavy to handle. Cain and Abel. The old Bible provides an object lesson here in the non-human, the creatures who according to evolutionary hierarchy go back too far to have developed a morality.

Except that of survival.

If you thrust a toll highway through the centre of endemism, the great botanical marvel, n'swebu, and you gouge ten million tons of heavy minerals and eight million tons of ilmenite from the sea-sculpted landscape of sand dunes, isn't that the morality of survival. Isn't that to industrialise? And isn't industrialisation, exploitation (it's termed that only in its positive meaning) of our rich resources, for the development of the economy, the uplift of the poor. What is survival if not the end of poverty. It's been pledged at the third inauguration of democratic government: the end of poverty. And if Abel has to be thrown from the nest by Cain; isn't that for a greater survival. The eagle allows this to happen, its all-powerful wings cannot prevail against it. Survival. Ten dams for one delta seen from Space. Civilisation goes against nature, that's the credo for what I do, I am. Protect. Preserve. But is that the law of survival. You preserve, *Chief,* and you're the one who trusts nature? Co-existence in nature is limited brutally—Cain throws Abel out of the nest—among creatures of which we're an animal species. Knowledge come in the quarantine of the childhood garden that perhaps whatever civilisation does to destroy nature, nature will find its solution in a measure of time we don't have (the pamphlet informs that this area was a sea, uncountable time before the rocks were pushed upward), that knowledge doesn't go far enough. A cop-out. Civilisation as you see it in your opposition of nature to the Australians' mining, the ten dams in the Okavango—it's child's play, a fantasy, when you admit the pragmatism in nature. No use returning to the photograph reproduced of the piece of fluff, morsel of life that is Abel, and looking for a solution.

The family outing is over. Monday the four-wheel drive back to the wilderness with Derek, Thapelo, according to the week's plan of research to which there is never a final solution, ever. That's the condition on which the work goes on, will go on. Phambili.

Benni was approaching, in her face the questioning brightness of one who has been wondering where he's got to. Berenice's had enough of nature, then, is coming to suggest they go home.

But when up the rock she reaches him, she says nothing. Their attention is attracted by an intense shadow above the trees whose lighter shade and sunlight break up the solid outlines of his face and body and hers. The grand stunt of the eagles, there, maybe the courting display described in the pamphlet.

The eagles have lifted away to their higher altitudes. The branches obscure viewing.

She has taken a step down, from him, backwards.

—Paul—

A signal for him to follow; he hands her the pamphlet, souvenir.

—I'm pregnant. Another child.—

—How did that happen.—

She shakes her head tenderly, in guilt. It's not because she tried another man, the cruelty he sees, of that solution. —I didn't tell you, but I haven't been taking any precaution.—

—So. For how long.— If the roving cells had continued to survive in his body, they could have disappeared by now, the pilot light of deadly radiance that he believed pursued them, could have gone out.

—Only the last two months.—

—So. What do you want to do.—

—Want to tell you.—

'So': it means there is an alternative he wants, abortion.

If Berenice would crumple into tears, effective in TV imagist resolution of confrontation, Benni waited steadily, only her hands came up, the fingers interlaced and her chin rested on this fist of—supplication, defiance.

He did not jump down to embrace her he stretched out his hand the palm wide the fingers spaced and curved and her hand came from support of her face to meet his grasp as if she were to be pulled from a foundering boat or a landfall.

Not an epiphany, life moves more slowly and inexorably than any belief in that. Except there's the question of why she chose that moment and place to announce herself. Well. Did she think, was she given courage (what a bastard to have said, Get yourself another man), the telling of the abortion of Abel from the nest made time and place propitiate, for the right perception.

Lyndsay was told. A sibling for Nicholas. Although he was not so much an only child now that Klara was—an unexpected form of relationship, unnamed, as she had been. Lyndsay herself doesn't define it, the child has not been taught to call her mama, or should it be grandma—that's the question but not a problem: she's Lyndsay to the child, and this doesn't undermine authority; or what looks like love, apparently.

Benni is overwhelmingly energetic, working in her advancing position at the Agency to take advantage of the improvement in the economy, as beautiful as ever, the face above the thickening body. When gestation is over (difficult not to think in terms of the vocabulary familiar for the other mammals that should be saved from extinction) will be the time to judge. If what is born is not affected, mutated in some way by sperm spurted from a body that had emanated radiance. Only then. In the meantime have to trust. What? Benni's instinct. Her contribution to starting over in a new state of existence. She has had a scan which reveals the curled-up foetus has male genitals already formed. A son. Be able to think of this being as a son when other things have been verified. You can be guilty of what you were not responsible for. Derek and Thapelo are congratulatory when they notice, on Sunday lunch invitations, the mound his wife carries under her flowing robe (Berenice's flair has taken to African dress as most attractive, in her present shape). Their jubilation—did they think a man wouldn't be able to make it after the state of quarantine—is infectious, it calls for a few beers Thapelo contributes to be enjoyed with rations in the wilderness. Nickie's hand is taken by his mother and placed on her belly; your little brother's waiting in there. He won't be as big as me. Everyone laughs at the premature one-upmanship. But there is a gleaming joy of curiosity and anticipation that may be what will banish for good the fingers forced from the iron gate, *Daddy! Paul!* Klara hears she too will have a little brother. Why not? A family has to be constituted for one who has none. She has been introduced to Jacqueline, the one of Paul's sisters who lives in the city, not Brazil or on an ostrich farm. Jacqueline's adolescent daughters make a great fuss of the little girl, putting bangles on her arms and bows on her dreadlocks. Likely Lyndsay may have told the prospective grandfather of the new addition expected by his son, in one of the occasional letters to Stavanger. No response to Paul and Benni, from there. If the father writes to her, the mother doesn't bring letters to the family, any more; the absence is not noted, perhaps not noticed, Klara and Nickie are playing a wild game, friends are expected. Lyndsay has sat for the first time in her judge's robes, at her elevation in court. If she's mentioned that, he must be allowed to be proud of her. Still.

Lyndsay came with a letter again one day, without the accompanying happening of the child, and after calling to ask if he was alone. Yes, his wife Benni couldn't forego a promotional cocktail party which Berenice should host despite the hard swell under the beaded African robe that announced, in medical jargon, her term was approaching.

His mother ignored Nickie watching the children's television programme he demanded with Benni's inherited charm. Taking it out of a courier's plastic packet she, once more, gave over the letter. The son found the envelope unopened—uncomprehending, ready to be irritated, what's this for, Ma, looked away from her. The address: the writing unfamiliar.

He slit the top of the envelope carefully and drew out the folded sheet at the same time handing it towards her, but she came to stand close beside him, head bent to read it together.

Stavanger.

Lyndsay recognised the handwriting from the statement of expenses the guide had presented at the end of each week of services in Mexico. She sensed her lips moving as she and her son read, as if following a foreign language. Dear Mrs Bannerman, I didn't want to shock over the phone, so I write to tell you he died last night, Adrian. In his sleep, the doctor came at once, I called. It was heart failure. He did not suffer. It was after the theatre. We had a nice walk by the sea in the afternoon. That was yesterday, 14th. So that was the date when it happened.

Both stopped reading. What happened: he stayed behind in Mexico, he went to Norway. Gone away. It is difficult to re-alise another departure. If this had been a letter from Adrian telling at last that he was not coming back, the state of re-tirement he was in, Stavanger, was final, would that have been different? But what an insane escapist thought. Even if they were having it together. Adrian is dead. He hasn't an-nounced finality. He's silent about it. Lyndsay and he read poetry together when they were young, tags remain, 'Death is silence, things which are not'. The guide he retired to speaks, writes for him.

Her son—their son—stirs the sheet of paper; they must read on. As if there is anything to say. Already told: died in his sleep, in bed beside the guide of course, no suffering, she knows because she was there, she simply sensed there was no rise and fall of breath or his body was cold against hers. They had walked together in the afternoon on the beautiful North Sea beach, Sola, a theatre where the streak of wet in the light from the stage that touched his cheek announced another kind of grief.

Read on. A gap, a pause at the word processor before a new start to this letter. Mrs Bannerman (again, though surely thought of as Lyndsay, embarrassment, guilt at the appropriation of retirement or late assurance that this title of marriage would never have been usurped) Mrs Bannerman, I have made all the enquiries, I will do it immediately you give me details where he must be received. My telephone number and email is at the top of the page. I can arrange it. I will send his body.

Smiling.

How else. In the grief she also must feel.

They walk into early evening light in the garden of Paul's house, to which he returned from that other garden. Up and down, slowly, legs move even if mind doesn't. To the shrubs and the acacia where the children's swings hang twinned, one's been strung up for Klara too; and back. Lyndsay trips over an abandoned toy in the rapid rise of darkness in Africa and he steadies her; also himself, to speak. Silence is only for the dead. Adrian.

Let's go in.

It's no-one else's decision, only theirs, as the conditions of another state of existence were finally between them alone in quarantine. He doesn't dutifully indicate, it's yours to decide, you, his lover, that indefinable relation dubbed by law and church, wife. Do you want him back; if dead. Did he ever express that primeval urge, to be buried in his natal soil. The idea that his death in the logical sequence of events after retirement would happen elsewhere never occurred. He could have had a heart attack and died in the Arctic under the *aurora borealis*, that retirement venture with Lyndsay that didn't come off. Preserved in ice ready to be flown home.

Home. From Stavanger. Begin over again, from the grave. Or the ashes of the crematorium. There are new beginnings,

in place. This's not *home* you left to follow so late, in archaeological digs, your avocation.

Smiling.

Found it.

They didn't tell other members of the family, not Jacqueline, not Susan, not Emma in Brazil, of the offer. An email
was sent thanking the guide and declining. His mother asked
Paul to place his name alongside hers. He had his sense of
loss carried with him in the wilderness that still needed him
and his team, Derek, Thapelo, always new threats to which
there must be human solutions (if your father dies do you
now exist in his place, nature's solution). If there's a possibility for the dune mining project or the pebble-bed nuclear reactor to be outlawed that's proof that what is a vocation and
an avocation may be worth pursuing in the limited span of
one individual's minuscule existence, not seen from Space.

What she—Lyndsay—does with sorrow—it must be?—
cannot be asked and must not be pried at or spied upon. The
life of parents is a mystery even when you are paired off with
someone in a version of the state, yourself. She has her suc-
cesses, as the defeat of destruction of the Pondoland dunes, if
achieved, would be a success at least partly attributable to
Derek, Thapelo and himself. She's been appointed to serve
on the Constitutional Court, and this is no Gender Affirmative post, that's certain.

Adrian is not a taboo subject. Paul does not know that she
has on her desk in her office at the Constitutional Court a
photograph of Adrian she took when they were together at

an archaeological site in Mexico. They speak of Adrian when a context comes up to remember something he might have remarked, laughed at with them, and when listening to music together, talking of his depth of understanding from which she profited and, yes, Paul's evidently growing enjoyment must have come, even of those composers she's never learnt to listen to without a sense of psychic disruption, Stockhausen, Penderecki etcetera. Perhaps the only way to break the silence is to have passed on something. Impalpable.

A well-secured box addressed in the same unfamiliar hand eventually was delivered, containing a few small archaeological artifacts, a reproduction feather headdress of the kind seen being made with delicate ancestral skill by vendors outside the Museum of Anthropology, and what was evidently a draft of thoughts on the experience of seeing unearthed accomplishments of the ancient past when you belong to an era where there are wars going on over who possesses weapons that could destroy all trace of it. She gave the artifacts, headdress, and the manuscript to the Department of Archaeology at a university where one of the academics was a friend. She asked, maybe the university press would publish the draft in some form.

EDEN OF AFRICA FACING THREAT OF
BEING SUBMERGED BY FLOODS

This is the kind of lyrical drama a newspaper headline makes of the waters Noah must have seen. But not from Outer Space. Not from a helicopter. The team has come back from a second survey of Okavango to map-covered walls, spread aerial photographs and half-drunk cups of instant coffee. Which is the reality? Here or there. It's not normal to live in two environments, every traveller knows the disorientation, disbelief, that is the brief consequence of leaving home and walking out into a foreign country ten hours later. But this consequence of being back among domestic objects and four walls, from wilderness, earth or water is a condition of living, not jet lag.

As they go over in their minds and talk what was seen down below, the observations shouted, half-heard, to one another against the racket of the helicopter, there is another question of which is the reality: the 'Eden' treasure feared threatened or the people of the central delta there, told they must abandon their homes before the rising waters. What's going to happen to them anyway, if ten dams that will alter the cosmic picture of the world as seen from Space are built?

Shouldn't be thinking about this, like this. The practice of conservation, boots in the mud, Thapelo's occasional addition of beers to basic supplies, concentrates on one issue at a time, some sort of sequence in activity while the commissions keep sitting, for or against. What is in the others' minds—about these people.

Derek's glance moves down a newspaper cutting that had reported interviews with the Delta people about the dams. —No-one will evict us from our ancestral lands. It is a gift from God, and our forefathers' soil.—

How does this emotional stuff, no doubt genuine as many (hopeless) defences are (isn't that the principle of rousing the Amadiba over the effects of the toll highway), strike Thapelo? He's one of those all over Africa who were long ago evicted from the forefathers' soil. And even what was left to them was 'a gift from God', the white man's God, not the ancestral ones? 'God': the first colonial civilising dispensation, a token something of a whole country dispossessed.

Thapelo needs none of his white mates' tact; seventeen months in solitary detention in the bad old days and none of the Gods did anything about it. He smiles and lifts his fingers softly up, down, from where his hands rest on the table, saluting respect to the ancestors but in acceptance of realities. His people have had to abandon their homes so many times and not for reasons of their safety before a flood.

—Safari guides report animals have drowned; we didn't see any bodies floating.—

—Didn't fly low enough and they might be caught in the submerged reeds and stuff.—

—An elephant? Submerged?—

—Doesn't mention the big guys.—

There's a season of flood, at expected levels, part of the ecological balance dealing with the salts, every year. But such extensive and unusual waters; a great inundation. Copies of backgound documents are handed round. An expert geoscientist, McCarthy, has found—predicts?—that after about 150 years toxic salts will destroy all plants (Derek starts to read aloud and the other two shush him as they read for themselves) . . . and at this point the floodwaters should erode the islands and release salts into the swamp. But with perfect timing papyrus and hippo grass upstream will have encroached into channels, causing sand levels to rise and blocking their flow. (Silenced Derek glances up: Man, we know all that. The others won't be distracted: Chief, you never know it all.) The water is diverted elsewhere and the old islands dry out. Then in that mysterious way it does, the peat in these dry areas catches fire (somebody's god strikes a match?) creating a mosaic of burning forests up to fifteen centimetres deep . . . these wild fires can burn for decades, destroying all life growing above them. After the fires have died, summer rains flush saline poisons deep below ground. Nutrients from the fires combine to form fertile soils . . . in this way the flow of water and creation of islands is constantly changing . . . the entire organism named Okavango renews itself.

Splendid, triumphant. Wola! Cho! Jabula! Phambili! Only the exclamations picked up from Thapelo's languages are adequate. The Okavango's revenge. Originating hundreds of kilometres away, every year with the spring rains the rivers Cuebe,

Longa, Custi, Cichi, Cubango—Africa-named before the white men dubbed them with that other reality, discovery for Europe—send a pulse of water, no, now a magnificent flood, the perennial wetland becomes a high waterland (what does it look like from Space!). Drowns projects, obliterates the idea of ten dams. And carries its own knowledge of dispersal, subsidence, knowledge of its own means of renewal in time.

Read on. However there is a problem against which the living swamp has not had time to develop a defence: humans.

The intention to build ten dams is not submerged.

So what is the reality. The human reality, Chief, Bra, however you're seen or you see yourself, the immediate, market reality—that's what counts in what you learn from the mother of your children, one in the womb, is the real world. Okavango left to itself will renew eternally. That is: woah!—eternity also has to be defined: as long as the earth is not ended by explosions of irreversible radiance. People don't live eternity; they live a finite Now. The mining of the dunes. Now the Australians have made a deal with a fifty-one percent black-owned company. The blacks are to have a fifteen percent share in the dunes mining project. While we were busy working with the International Rivers Network, the World Conservation Union, the Wild Life and Environmental Society, all our good acronym partners, the Aussies were spending nine months, same gestation period as the human ovum fertilised by a radiance survivor's sperm, negotiating this agreement which—confidently—now will allow to be granted from the Government a prospecting permit for the eighty-nine million rands, around eight million pounds, international enterprises may be quoted in many currencies, to proceed. That's the official-speak to express it, 'Allow to be granted'. A worthy incentive isn't a bribe, my Bra. No-one can disagree with the necessity for blacks to enter the development economy at a major level, fifteen percent is a good start? Thapelo gives a grand fanfaring laugh, for celebration or derision: is it yona ke yona or shaya-shaya, this bit of black empowerment? There's also the concomitant reality that a toll highway carrying the derived minerals and ilmenite (used in the fabric and the beauty business, cosmetic industries) to a smelter and processor in the city centuries ago named by homesick Europeans 'East London', might bring a weekly wage to replace the sacrifice, God's gift of a few crop fields, unique endemism, and twenty-two kilometres of sand dunes which used to be fished from instead of mined. Bring hi-fi systems and cars. Yes! Easy to sneer at materialism and its Agency seductions while existence within it has the luxury of dissatisfaction, the wilderness to oppose it.

Who's to decide.

This kind of research has no place in this room with two mates—we just happen to be earth-brothers if not blood-brothers—Thapelo and Derek with whom is shared what the self pursues as reality. She. Benni, it must be allowed, is the other reality. Berenice. Hers, chosen, or advised by its effectiveness in the finite. Get a life! The Agency admonishment.

This kind of subject is left in the garden.

In quarantine.

Thapelo tips his chair, boots lifted, rights it with the flourish of impact to the floor loud before them.

A summons. He senses danger; distraction.

Benni's soft hand on his cheek against the prickle of morning's beard wakes him, her Berenice voice coaxingly calls his name. Half-returned, half in the other world of sleep, can't help receiving the calm purpose with which the female, like any in the wild, approaches what must be a cataleptic ordeal; the reverse of the invasion of the body by demonic light, the contrary, a desertion by what has been tenderly part of it, feeding from a common life-blood. She slides the African robe over her belly, ready to go to a birth-place here in the city, a clinic not a hide under bushes, but the purpose of shelter for the event is the same. It's something that cannot be shared. At least she understands he is not one to be a spectator, present. He's not the man who massaged her feet at the event of the first child.

In the meantime.
The floods have subsided. During the waiting period Queen

MaSobhuza Sigcau of Pondoland has told the press that em-
ployees of the sand dunes mining project were ordering people
in the area to 'vacate' their homes because preparations to
mine were beginning. They were given documents of agreement to sign; many are illiterate and some lost their cattle
and sheep as a result of being forced to move. There have been
different commands for this kind of thing. *Juden heraus.*
Take your choice. And our country's signed, ratified the
International Biodiversity Strategic Action Plan (what a
mouthful, nearly as difficult to spit out as to carry out)—
how's the Minister heading off to tell the World Convention
we're going to allow a four-lane highway through one of the
named hotspots of global diversity? You answer that one!
The answer comes. Vuka Mister Minister! Get a life! . . .
Well, at least we have to admit they've had to back down and
allow an appeal against their go-ahead for it . . . Haai!—
delaying tactics. Let the protestors get tired and fall asleep.
Meanwhile. The ten dams? All quiet right now but such cosmic plans get shelved, not torn up. And the Australians? Still
happy they're going to get the rubber stamp to take sixteen
million tons of titanium minerals plus eight millions of ilmenite out of the dunes; sure-sure prepared to hang in there
for it. The pebble-bed reactor? Needs something like ten
billions—what's that in dollars, pounds, euros—from foreign
investors to help out if it's to be built, but it's not abandoned— —No way, my man!— The 'feasibility' and 'safety'
of it are being 'continuously evaluated by the relevant Government Department'. *Voetsek, we don't want you.* Read it
aloud from the Stop Press edition. 'These were the harsh
words from environmental supporters, a delegation of the
Nuclear Energy Costs and the Earth Campaign gathered out-

side the British Trade Investment offices in Johannesburg today to hand over a memorandum denouncing British Nuclear Fuels as a "nightmare" investor in partnership with Eskom and the South African state-owned Industrial Development Corporation, a consortium to oversee commercialising of the pebble-bed modular reactor.' Meanwhile. The lapse of time medically decreed before the scan which would decide whether the body should again be irradiated, passed. All clear for the present; another scan, maybe, delayed for another decision.

The son has emerged to take on the world with all the necessary equipment, weapons—two arms, two hands, ten prehensile fingers, two legs, feet and toes (verify ten), the genitals which were already evident in the foetal scan, a shapely head and open eyes of profound indeterminate colour that are already reacting with the capacity of sight. The sperm of the radiant progenitor-survivor has achieved no distorting or crippling of the creation.

Destruction takes on many states of existence; on this one the predatory stare has gone out. Must invite Thapelo and Derek again for a couple of beers where there's new life confirmed.

Thapelo is first with exuberant confirmation of other news that had given off smoke signals to the waiting three, through their eavesdropping connections. Minister of Environmental Affairs, van Schalkwyk, has set aside (abandoned? a for real no-no? maybe) a decision made a year before this month of birth to construct the Pondoland Wild Coast toll road. And the Minister of Minerals and Energy, she's announced that the pebble-bed nuclear reactor is halted. 'Pending further environmental assessment'; yes—oh of course.

But what about the sand dunes, the titanium, the ilmenite for the pretty girls' make-up, my brothers!

Final licence of destruction must never be admitted, granted. That's the creed. Work to be done. Yona ke yona. This is it. Phambili. There's a half-triumphal burst of laughter to be shared.

Wet the baby's head! Derek toasts.

Glossary

ayeye	An expression teasing someone for his faults
braai	A barbecue
bundu	The bush; nowhere
cho!	A greeting calling attention to something
eish	An expression of reluctance
jabula	Be happy
khan'da	Operate; scheme
lalela	Listen
makhosi	Tribal chiefs; traditional leaders
n'swebu	Marvellous
phambili	Come on; go for it
sangoma	Traditional healer
shaya-shaya	A deliberately false statement
tsotsi	Street gangster
tuka	A long time ago
voetsek	Get out; push off
vuka	Wake up
wola	Hi
woza	Rise
yebo	A greeting, or affirmation
yona ke yona	This is it

FOR MORE WORKS BY NOBEL PRIZE–WINNER NADINE GORDIMER, LOOK FOR THE

> "The symbols Nadine Gordimer holds up
> are good for all times and all places, reminding
> us of our universal humanity."
> —*New York Herald Tribune*

The Pickup

A riveting story of a passionate love affair that begins as a casual encounter between a rich, white South African girl and an illegal Arab immigrant. A novel of great power, psychological surprises, and unexpected turns, *The Pickup* is "a masterpiece of creative empathy . . . a gripping tale of contemporary anguish and unexpected desire" (Edward Said).   *ISBN 0-14-200142-2*

My Son's Story

Told through the eyes of a young man, this is the story of what he knows and what he imagines of political and erotic liberation, of sexual jealousy between father and adolescent son, and of the power of apartheid behind the changes in 1980s South Africa.

"In *My Son's Story*, Nadine Gordimer has given us a world of bleak beauty and enormous force."   —*The Washington Post Book World*
ISBN 0 14-015975-4

Jump and Other Short Stories

In sixteen stories ranging from the dynamics of family life to the worldwide confusion of human values, Nadine Gordimer gives us access to many lives in places from exotic Mozambique to turbulent South Africa. Moving, incisive, and with strong moral resonance, Gordimer's stories offer a portrait of life as it is lived at the end of the twentieth century.   *ISBN 0-14-016534-7*

July's People

As South Africa turns into a raging battleground between blacks and whites, the liberal white Smales family members are led to refuge by their servant, July. What happens to them—the shifts in character and relationships—provides an unforgettable look into the terrifying tacit understanding and misunderstanding between blacks and whites.
ISBN 0-14-006140-1

Burger's Daughter
This brilliantly realized work unfolds the story of a young woman's slowly evolving identity in the turbulent political environment of South Africa. Her father's death in prison leaves Rosa moving through an overwhelming flood of sensuously described memories that will not release her until she arrives at last at a fresh understanding of her life, sweeping this engrossing narrative to a triumphant conclusion.
ISBN 0-14-005593-2

The Conservationist
Mehring is rich. He has all the privileges and possessions that South Africa has to offer, but his possessions refuse to remain objects. His wife, son, and mistress leave him; his foreman and workers become increasingly indifferent to his stewardship; even the land rises up, as drought, then flood, destroys his farm.
ISBN 0-14-004716-6

The House Gun
A house gun—something kept like a house cat in post-apartheid South Africa, a fact of ordinary life at the end of the last century where violence was in the air. *The House Gun* is a passionate narrative of that final test of complex human relations we call love, moving from the intimate to the general condition. If it is a parable of violence it is also an affirmation of the will to reconcile that starts where it must, between individual men and women.
ISBN 0-14-027820-6

Loot and Other Stories
With her characteristic brilliance, in ten stories Gordimer follows the inner lives of characters confronted by unforeseen circumstances. An earthquake offers tragedy and opportunity in the title story; "Mission Statement" describes a bureaucrat's idealism, the ghosts of colonial history, and a love affair that ends astoundingly; and in "Karma," a disembodied narrator questions the nature of existence in five returns to earthly life. Revelatory and powerful, these are stories that challenge our deepest convictions even as they dazzle us with their artful lyricism.
ISBN 0-14-200468-5

None to Accompany Me
In an extraordinary period immediately before the first nonracial election and the beginning of majority rule in South Africa, Vera Stark works as a lawyer representing blacks in the struggle to reclaim the land. The return of exiles is transforming the city, and through the lives of Didymus Maqoma, his wife Sibongile, and their lovely daughter who cannot even speak her parents' African language, the reader experiences the strange passions, reversals, and dangers that accompany new won access to power.
ISBN 0-14-025039-5

FOR THE BEST IN PAPERBACKS, LOOK FOR THE

In every corner of the world, on every subject under the sun, Penguin represents quality and variety—the very best in publishing today.

For complete information about books available from Penguin—including Penguin Classics, Penguin Compass, and Puffins—and how to order them, write to us at the appropriate address below. Please note that for copyright reasons the selection of books varies from country to country.

In the United States: Please write to *Penguin Group (USA), P.O. Box 12289 Dept. B, Newark, New Jersey 07101-5289* or call 1-800-788-6262.

In the United Kingdom: Please write to *Dept. EP, Penguin Books Ltd, Bath Road, Harmondsworth, West Drayton, Middlesex UB7 0DA.*

In Canada: Please write to *Penguin Books Canada Ltd, 90 Eglinton Avenue East, Suite 700, Toronto, Ontario M4P 2Y3.*

In Australia: Please write to *Penguin Books Australia Ltd, P.O. Box 257, Ringwood, Victoria 3134.*

In New Zealand: Please write to *Penguin Books (NZ) Ltd, Private Bag 102902, North Shore Mail Centre, Auckland 10.*

In India: Please write to *Penguin Books India Pvt Ltd, 11 Panchsheel Shopping Centre, Panchsheel Park, New Delhi 110 017.*

In the Netherlands: Please write to *Penguin Books Netherlands bv, Postbus 3507, NL-1001 AH Amsterdam.*

In Germany: Please write to *Penguin Books Deutschland GmbH, Metzlerstrasse 26, 60594 Frankfurt am Main.*

In Spain: Please write to *Penguin Books S. A., Bravo Murillo 19, 1° B, 28015 Madrid.*

In Italy: Please write to *Penguin Italia s.r.l., Via Benedetto Croce 2, 20094 Corsico, Milano.*

In France: Please write to *Penguin France, Le Carré Wilson, 62 rue Benjamin Baillaud, 31500 Toulouse.*

In Japan: Please write to *Penguin Books Japan Ltd, Kaneko Building, 2-3-25 Koraku, Bunkyo-Ku, Tokyo 112.*

In South Africa: Please write to *Penguin Books South Africa (Pty) Ltd, Private Bag X14, Parkview, 2122 Johannesburg.*